Unplugged
Clark Randolph

To Elizabeth—

> A million thanks for encouraging me to write this story that began as a thought in my mind to the final word typed with my computer. Your love, support and encouragement makes me want to write each and every day for you. Here's to a book that catches your eye as you pass by it on the shelf.

To Dino—

> You perished while trying your best to protect my home. I won't ever forget you, and may you live on as a literary hero for many years to come.

Love is God. God is love. Those who are close to God preserve and protect their love. Love requires commitment and dedication. That takes time.

Sexual love demands appointments. Love is kind, light and lovely. We begin by being loved by our parents. To lose that love is evidence of a lost childhood.

Puppy love is pure and safe.

As we grow older, love looks back over our lives—and forward—in the form of grandchildren. Love is wisdom.

Helping people extends one's love. Ultimately, we meet love again in the form of God.

Love is love of yourself. True love is unconditional. No matter what you do, you are loved.

We love our pets and they love us in return.

Friendship is a form of love.

Love is a warm puppy.

Love is warm, sometimes hot.

Love unites nations. The Bible says love thy enemy. Love makes the world go round.

Love is sunshine. Love is the majesty of mountains. Love is a blue sky. Love is the first snowflake.

Love is a rainbow. Love is red hot, cool blue, sunny yellow, the green of new leaves the royalty of purple.

A mother's love is great. A father's love is strong.

Love is feeling safe.

—Mary Alice Covington

Chapter 1: Hello Sandra's Family

With all its might, a snow white Maltese puppy leaped from the floor to the summit of the lump in the bed that was far from awake, swinging a fiercely moving tail directly into the face of Caroline Hempheart. As the dog wagged away in excitement, Caroline took a punishing combination of tail wags to the face, and puppy paws to the abdomen forced her to sit up straight, look the Maltese straight in the eyes, and scream, "Becker, it's not time to wake up yet!"

The simple acknowledgement of the dog's name was enough to keep the Maltese wagging and jumping away on Caroline's fragile body for as many minutes as was needed to alert Caroline that this dog had to use the bathroom right now.

Caroline slowly rose from her slumber, finding the first pair of flip flops she could locate to slide on her feet as she searched for a clip or anything that could hold up the seemingly unending amount of hair that was pointing in every direction from her head.

"Becks, what time is it? Why are you so disrespectful right now? Can't you see I am trying to sleep?" Caroline yelped out in a mix of words and morning mumbling that utterly confused the young Maltese.

After folding her hair into a clip that was previously used to keep potato chips fresh, she tossed on a rainbow sweatshirt that her lesbian friend, Melissa, had left behind a few nights earlier and some pink shorts that read "Mountain Middle" on the butt, which she'd had since the sixth grade. Armed with Becker's leash, she clasped the leopard print collar to Becker's now gyrating head and clicked the leash on tight, guiding the dog to the door as she gripped for her keys off the nightstand at the last minute before exiting the room for the staircase.

Rumbling down the dark staircase and hearing a steady flow of adult conversation coming from the ground floor, a sudden image flashed into Caroline's head of her boyfriend's entire family gathered in the living room of her house waiting for her to go to Sunday brunch.

It couldn't be. There is no way they'd be here. Cam is out of town on a fishing trip; they wouldn't have come without him. I'm just hearing stuff, Caroline thought to herself as Becker pushed for a faster approach to the bottom of the staircase.

"Thank goodness," she sighed, as she reached the bottom of the narrow staircase with Becker in tow. "It's only my roommate's entire family that gets to see me like this," Caroline grumbled as her roommate Sandra's entire family sat patiently waiting in the various living room furniture that had been collected from the myriad of thrift stores around their college town.

There was Mandy, the stuck-up sister of her roommate, Sandra, and Cindy, the aunt that advocated for Sandra to live alone in order to stay away from the temptations of college life, and Bob, the controlling father that had forced Sandra to major in biology since he thought she should be a doctor. And of course, the mother—the mother of them all, Hope Reynolds sat patiently disturbed, obviously not pleased with her daughter's tardiness, now welcoming the chance to see Caroline at her worst.

"Hi Caroline. I hope we did not wake you?" politely came from the mouth of Hope Reynolds, cosigner of her current house lease.

"No, no, don't be silly. I've been studying for hours up there. I just figured Becker needed a walk. Everything is great—good to see you all," Caroline embarrassingly said as she took the goo from her eyes and gently placed it on the side of her shorts in an effort to be somewhat believable in her claim to have been awake for hours upstairs.

Caroline's heart began to beat faster and faster until she felt like she could faint right there on the spot. She hated being seen unkept, and this little family reunion of Sandra's should've been cleared with her prior to their arrival. What if she had come down in her Princess Bride pajamas, she wondered, as she exited the home with the ever-jubilant Maltese, Becker, the chip clip in her hair clanking against the doorway as she walked out.

Chapter 2: The Two-Beer Job

Navigating the rock path that lay in front of her, Caroline moved swiftly from one stepping stone to the next, making sure not to veer off the stones in fear of stepping in Becker's past offerings. As she approached the street, her head continued to sway from side to side as if she hadn't really just gone through that embarrassing moment with her roommate's family. She vowed to forget it ever happened, and to conveniently stay out walking good old Becker long enough that by the time she returned to the house the circus would be gone.

"Caroline, is that you?" shouted a burly man from the driver's side window of a slow-moving pickup truck painted Redneck blue.

Caroline looked down to the ground, pretending not to hear the sole driver on the empty street that just abruptly yelled her name out loud.

"Hey, Caroline, it's Todd. What are you doing over there?" the man shouted as he guided his truck closer to where she was now standing, arms folded clinching Becker's leash tightly in a ball with her fist.

"Hi Todd, what are you doing over here? Shouldn't you be up in a tree with a mouthful of disgusting, mud-looking tobacco in your mouth sniffing out the reindeers or whatever you hunting types like to do on a nice Sunday morning like this one?" Caroline said as she braced for the oncoming array of jokes about her appearance.

"No, no, we don't hunt reindeer. We hunt regular deer—you know, bucks," Todd calmly explained as he pulled up to within three feet of Caroline, putting his foot on the brakes as if to show he was stopping, but not for long.

"I see, thanks for pointing that out. Well, it's good to see you, Todd. I'm just here walking my pal Becker before I head out to the library to work on that sociology assignment we have due tomorrow," Caroline said.

Todd glanced at Caroline with an inquisitive look, figuring out that she was in fact in the same sociology class, and that she was in fact talking about an assignment that apparently was nearing its due date.

"Oh, yeah, that. I should be banging that assignment out at about 11 o'clock tonight. I figure it's a two-beer job," Todd said, staring directly at Caroline's sweatshirt.

"A two-beer job?" Caroline hesitantly asked as if she really didn't want to know the answer.

"Yep, as in it'll take about two beers for me to get it done—one beer for the part about the reading, and one beer for the part about the writing," Todd explained confidently as if he were referring to a nightly ritual performed by even the studious of academics.

Before Caroline could remark on this obviously flawed study habit, a large white SUV appeared in Todd's rearview mirror, approaching with a continuous chorus of air horn blows that made them both cover their ears in pain.

"I've got to go, gal. I'll see you tomorrow in class. That's Ricky behind us and apparently he's ready to go now," Todd explained as he let his foot off the brake enough to allow his pickup to cut in front of the white SUV and speed away down the road at a rapidly increasing pace.

Caroline released a considerable amount of slack from Becker's leash and continued her stroll down the street.

The sun-drenched morning spoke to Caroline's anxiety, allowing her to calm down and realize that everything she had been upset about earlier meant nothing. As Becker's pace slowed, Caroline's feet slowed as well, allowing her to maintain a still moment of thought for minutes at a time without moving a muscle.

What was different today, she wondered. What made her feel like something was going to change in her life in the very near future, Caroline wondered as she shot a blank stare to a passing car.

Coffee. She realized a cup of coffee would be the perfect resolution to this strange emotion that predicted a change in her future. She thought of her friend, Beth Rigby, that got sick of her life one day and moved to Montana for six months to herd cattle. Beth had been one of the more superficial people Caroline had ever met, and it boggled her mind to think of her in overalls, boots and a cowboy hat.

Caroline knew she wouldn't be herding steer anytime soon; it was the other life changing possibilities that had her mind going at a million miles an hour. Coffee—it was time for a big bold cup of it.

Chapter 3: Thanks, Peanut Head

"One extra large cup of the bold please," Caroline shouted to the clerk of Nutty Buddy Coffee Palace, the only coffee shop located within 20 miles of her small, rural Ohio college campus.

"Cream, sugar or the works?" asked the attendant in a black coffee bean suit with a large foam peanut on his head.

"Two creams and two sugars please," Caroline shouted back at the man as the crowds continued to swell in front of the now-overwhelmed peanut head.

Caroline rested her car keys on the counter as she watched the man take a giant cup akin to those 40-ounce souvenir cups overweight people buy at sporting events and fill it with a mix of black coffee and a sugary milky substance. Caroline's eyes became fixed on the large straw of the cup that was built into the design, with a fat enough width to fit way too much liquid through it at one time.

"Here you are. Please be careful, this beverage is hot," the attendant explained to Caroline as he passed off the coffee goblet, giving her a look like she had been warned that the giant steaming cup of coffee was, in fact, hot.

Caroline thanked the man as she took both hands to the

massive cup and made her way through the mix of Mason Smith University students and Thomasville locals that frequented the establishment after church.

The Nutty Buddy Coffee Palace was located on Main Street in the heart of downtown Thomasville, Ohio. Thomasville, Ohio, was a town of great juxtaposition. The small liberal arts school Mason Smith University was primarily comprised of students that came from highly affluent families that could afford the $48,000 tuition bill each year. The few students that attended the school that weren't financially well off were numb enough to the idea of amassing large debt to sign on to financial aid packages that left the average graduate with nearly $100,000 in debt. Yet the local residents that weren't enrolled at MSU were poor—most never graduated from high school, nonetheless college.

Race, while not often talked about in Thomasville, also was at the heart of many town tensions. Most students at Mason Smith University were White, Asian or Pakistani. The campus would've been primarily all White if it weren't for MSU's global scholarship program that reached out to Pakistan's best and brightest with full tuition and the promise of a true American college experience in the heart of the Midwest, as the MSU global scholarship booklet spelled out.

Thomasville's local population was as Black as it was Hispanic as it was White. This racial blend played into the very threads of the town's fragile cloth. Since the college was the biggest employer in the town, it was often the case that the minorities would be the ones serving the student body that was primarily comprised of the future rich White elite, leading to local folks often looking at the students as elitist pricks, and the students looking at the locals as the help, rather than their equals.

What was the works, is that when they put peanuts in your coffee, how gross, Caroline thought to herself as she wandered to a table in the back of the square, one-room store.

"Is anyone sitting at this table?" Caroline asked a young gentleman feverishly tapping on the keys of his laptop.

"Nope, the seat is yours," the man said as he adjusted his power cord just enough to let Caroline's narrow frame slip between him and the adjacent table, where she plopped down with her coffee and looked up as if to find whatever answer she had come searching for.

"You gay?" asked the young gentleman that now had his laptop turned off and his full attention on Caroline.

"No, it's not my sweatshirt. This girl left it at my place the other night," Caroline explained while she tensed her shoulders enough to create a makeshift shrug.

"Oh, cool, you are just into experimenting. That's cool—me, too," the young man explained to Caroline as she stood up and walked toward the door.

Stupid. Why are you so stupid? Go home and change your clothing, Caroline thought to herself as she took her extra large coffee out the door of the Nutty Buddy Palace and headed for her car.

Chapter 4: Sip, Clip, Sip, Clip

Pushing the gigantic coffee mug against the door with her shoulder allowed Caroline to free up her hands enough to grab her keys from the pocket of her shorts. Fumbling the keys in her hands while keeping the focused look of an acrobat on a tight rope, Caroline found the right key, inserted it into the lock, and opened the door to her home.

"Hey thirsty girl, what's good?" immediately announced Caroline's roommate, Sandra, who lay chest down on the floor in a pool of newspaper inserts and rubber bands.

"Hi, what are you doing?" Caroline said with a quick glance to Sandra's now distracted eyes.

"I am trying to compare these two coupons for canned string beans to see which one is a better deal." Sandra said with an academic cadence that was usually reserved for science class.

"Oh, I didn't know you got the paper today. I'd love to read it after you're done clipping," Caroline noted as she walked closer to Sandra.

"This isn't today's paper; it's last week's paper. Tony at the Fast Stop down the street gives me last week's Sunday paper free if he has any left. Today he had some left!" Sandra said as a smile grew on her face.

Incredible, Caroline thought to herself as she walked past Sandra to find an open seat on the old brown sofa where she sat down, kicking her feet up on the old wood coffee table in front of her.

Sandra was one of the thriftiest people Caroline had ever encountered. Sandra constantly was trying to save money as if she had none, which of course was not the case, as her family seemed to own every farm in southern Ohio. It was more of a game for Sandra than it was practical, Caroline would often think as she watched Sandra indulge her inner cheapskate time and time again.

"Yeah, right before you got here I found this one coupon that gives you a free bag of Ruffles when you buy one at regular price. You eat Ruffles, if I recall correctly. Were you planning on buying any in the near future?" Sandra inquired, gently raising her eyebrow enough to accent her question with an odd facial expression.

"Nope, no Ruffles bag buying for me today. I know you'd love to get a free bag at my expense, but I actually have a big sociology assignment due tomorrow that I've got to get studying for," Caroline said with an increased volume to show Sandra she wasn't in the mood to kid around.

"OK, fair enough. I was just letting you know about an opportunity I had encountered. If you don't want to get in on it, that is fine with me," Sandra retorted.

The two of them sat quietly for several minutes, allowing several more coupons to be clipped from the week-old newspaper and at least 10 mighty sips from the giant coffee mug. A gentle rhythm started to emerge from the living room—a melody comprised of sip, clip, sip, clip, sip, clip—and it soothed them both.

Several more minutes passed and Caroline decided it was time to get ready for the library; she quietly headed upstairs to her room.

The door to Caroline's room swung open with a modest push from Caroline, and as soon as the door was set in motion, so was young Becker, jumping on Caroline's legs as if she had been gone for years and was finally back to greet her long lost friend.

"Calm down, Becks, you are going to get this coffee all over the place," Caroline barked at the dog, only to receive a slew of barks in return.

"Yes, it is good to see you, my white furry friend. It is good to see you," Caroline said as she rubbed the warm belly of Becker while she positioned her mega mug of coffee on the nearby bookshelf for safety.

Caroline waded through the sea of clothes that dotted her floor like leaves off an old tree in the middle of October. Clothing everywhere was spread about her room with a sprinkling of books for her college classes and an occasional Glamour magazine.

Caroline's feet tiptoed around, finding the few spots of exposed carpet to step on between the clothing, while Becker followed and ignored all the rules of walking in Caroline's room by stepping on any clothing that got in the dog's way.

The old maroon office chair that would look more appropriate in an accountant's office from the 1960s was turned away from the desk that held Caroline's laptop. She grasped the corner of the chair to spin it in her direction, falling into the indented cushion and rolling the chair to a front and center position in front of the desk. Caroline flipped her laptop's screen up and clicked the power button; it was time to check her e-mail.

After a few key taps, Caroline was logged into her e-mail

account, which she had not checked all weekend.

The inbox displayed five new messages that Caroline browsed through slowly so as to prolong her inevitable sociology homework.

Each message seemed more ridiculous than the next, starting with the first message in Caroline's inbox urging her to lose weight with an ancient ginger root treatment.

What a joke, Caroline thought as she deleted the message. The next message, find love in 60 seconds, Caroline thought for a minute about clicking the link, just to see what this sender defined as love, but decided to be a good girl and click delete.

The third e-mail startled her enough to sit up straight in her chair—a message from the university.

Finally, an e-mail worth reading, Caroline thought as she navigated the screen to the e-mail titled Important Notice from The Office of Financial Aid.

Caroline hoped it was good news about a new scholarship she had applied for a few months prior.

The news was not positive, and many would wonder how it could, in fact, end up in an inbox instead of being told face to face to begin with.

Caroline's eyes tripled in size as her head started to sway back and forth as if to reject what she had just read on the screen. Caroline's now bulging eyes erupted in tears while her body started to shake. She fell to the floor and laid still, her tears flowing from her face to the clothing on the floor as if she'd just learned of a death in the family, as if she'd just learned of something so tragic she couldn't even open her eyes.

Chapter 5: 38th Floor, Please

Ryan Todd lifted his umbrella just high enough to cover the stranger that stood at the stoplight with him entirely while still keeping his own body dry.

"Thanks, that is very kind of you," the stranger said to Ryan with a nod of approval.

"It's my pleasure. I bought a big umbrella for times just like this," Ryan yelled to the stranger next to him as the rain started to voraciously land all around them.

It was a cloudy, overcast, cold and downright uncomfortable Monday morning, and Ryan Todd was as happy as he thought he could be.

The stoplight turned to red, and the white outline of a person crossing the street illuminated 20 feet in front of them as they both walked out from under the umbrella and headed for the other end of the street.

Ryan's feet, nestled comfortably in $300 Italian leather loafers, skirted around puddles and potholes as he made his way across the street. Ryan leaped forward after hitting the sidewalk, hopping to safety underneath a towering office building that begged for legitimacy in a city full of towering office buildings.

After a quick shake of the umbrella and a tuck of the shirt,

Ryan briskly entered the large building's double glass doors that quietly shut behind him with the large and timeless typeface letters COLUMBUS TRIBUNE on them.

As fast as Ryan could manage without running he moved through the lobby of the building, passing by the statuesque security guards with a quick wave and a smile.

"How about those Knicks?" Ryan inquired to the now loose uniformed security guard standing by the elevator.

"They got lucky. They have a really awful starting five, I'll tell you that much. Their bench play is the only way they won that game," The security guard playfully remarked to Ryan as he entered the now open elevator doors.

"I'm telling you, they are going to the playoffs this year, and your Hawks are not!" Ryan stated as the doors to the elevator shut, leaving the security guard little time to respond.

The floors dinged off and lit up at a rate of every other second, allowing Ryan to catch his breath before arriving at the 38th floor where his office was located.

Ryan knew that he could let his mind wander until the fast-moving machine hit the 30th floor, then it was time for the game face.

In that brief minute of time, Ryan's face tightened as his mind wandered to a place it often went, a place that nobody else had ever known to exist in this young professional's mind, a serious and dark place.

Ding. The doors opened with precision speed, clanking against the frame when they were fully open as to alert the passenger that it was their time to depart.

Ryan walked swiftly through the newsroom of the Columbus Tribune, passing the junior reporters that nodded at him with admiration, past the sales manager and the general sales manager that cleverly pretended not to notice him even though their eyes immediately followed him once his back was to them. Ryan walked through the newsroom like he owned it, and in a small way, he did.

Chapter 6: Rich Guy Reporter

The mahogany wood desk sparkled with a minimalist shine as a yellow legal notepad, pen and shut laptop computer were the only things occupying the surface of the desk. Ryan reclined in his desk chair, rolling it back flush against the wall as he took in his anti-journalist office space. No clutter, no paper, no cubicle—this was a true anomaly in an industry that often thrived on and lived in chaos. The other incredible fact was that Ryan Todd, a baby-faced reporter from a well-to-do family, had come so far in the Columbus Tribune organization so soon.

Just a year earlier, Ryan was another number in a newsroom full of them. After graduating with honors from Ohio State University, Ryan landed a job that screamed entry level as much as any could. Ryan Todd was hired as the local business reporter, deputized with writing stories about local businesses in the Columbus region. His stories were so entry level, they didn't even make the paper's regional editions. Neither of his parents were able to read his stories since the Columbus Tribune they received at their door every morning was the Great Lakes edition, one that didn't include small tidbit stories like the ones Ryan so passionately wrote about.

There was the profile of a legend in the hot dog pedaling

business that showcased one man's struggle from homelessness to selling dozens of wieners on a bun to hungry downtown workers every week. Or the story about the window cleaning business that started using recycled toilet water in their cleaning solution to help save the earth. Ryan yearned to be more than just a young guy with a job; he wanted to be a force, he wanted to be in the middle of the fire.

Journalism was an obvious career path for Ryan. He was always good at writing. He loved to tell a story, and money was of no concern to him. Ryan always looked at a career as a way to stay busy, not as a means to putting food on the table.

His family was of modest means, his father working as a teacher and high school football coach, and his mother working as a nurse at the local hospital. From the outside looking in, the family looked like an average American middle-class family.

Ryan's grandfather on his dad's side, Bobby Todd, invented aluminum foil. An enterprising scientist with a knack for marketing, the man was able to amass a fortune before selling his aluminum foil brand and patents to the largest maker of household cleaning products for a price tag of more than $400 million in 1975.

Ryan had yet to be born, and yet his life was instantly altered nonetheless. As the sole child of Bobby Todd, Ryan's father Andrew Todd inherited a fortune larger than he could have ever imagined. In the 10 years after the sale of the company, Bobby Todd invested in a range of red hot companies that led him to nearly double his fortune before his death, leaving the entire fortune to his only son, Ryan's dad.

With little motivation to live a life of luxury, Andrew Todd created a trust for each of his children, even those that hadn't been born yet, and put most of the money into government-issued bonds. The Todds lived in a modest ranch house, drove a Ford Explorer, and kept their financial windfall as private as possible. Their suburban Cleveland town was safe, had quality schools, and offered the Todds an uncanny level of privacy. In towns like this one, a family with an average blue-collar income could easily afford a five-acre piece of property, complete with a dirt road as a driveway, and no neighbors in sight.

Ryan had a fairly normal upbringing. His family made a concerted effort to give him a normal life, full of normal Middle America things. Ryan drove a 15-year-old pickup truck in high school, shopped for clothing at the local mall, and when he wasn't playing football for his father worked at a local diner, making milkshakes for six bucks an hour.

Though Ryan knew the benefit of an ordinary life, and his mental stability was as good as it could be for someone his age, he always yearned for more. He always dreamed of the fancy car, the nice house with a pool, the trips to exotic places. He always dreamed of spending some of that aluminum foil money, and when he turned 21, that is just what he did.

With a nearly impeccable grade point average at Ohio State University and a girlfriend waiting for him to impress her, Ryan Todd was given control of his $40 million trust on March 2nd, 2003, his 21st birthday.

A black BMW six series convertible was the first thing Ryan purchased. It wasn't even available for another year, yet Ryan knew it was the car he wanted. A larger home outside of Columbus, Ohio, in the posh suburb of Worthington was next on the list, complete with the pool, hot tub and game room. Finally, it was time for the gadgets, and Ryan had them all—flat-screen televisions, portable computers, GPS receivers and mp3 players that could take your pulse when not playing your favorite music. If it was hot, Ryan had it. His neighbors thought he was a well-to-do businessperson that had earned his fortune. Little did they know it had nothing to do with Ryan's accomplishments.

While his parents did not necessarily approve of Ryan's spending, they were cautiously optimistic that this spending was just a phase, and if that was in fact that case, they were just glad he stayed close to home and didn't buy a plane or private island, or some other rich folk luxury that would bring more problems than happiness.

"What's up with the Conway Insurance fraud piece. Is that going to be ready for print this week?" Roland Smith, the senior editor of the Columbus Tribune, said to Ryan poking his head in the door, disrupting Ryan's peaceful nostalgia session.

"Oh, yes, I've got one more interview to do, and that'll be it. With luck, I'll have it in your inbox by tomorrow morning," Ryan explained to the editor, intentionally understating the projected time of completion, knowing the article was a few small edits from being finished.

"Great, I appreciate it, man," Ronald Smith said while glancing at Ryan's empty desk and walking away from his office door at the same time.

Ryan flipped open his laptop, letting his elbows fall to the desk. It was time to get to work.

Chapter 7: Should've Been a Finance Major

Ultimately, it came down to dropping out of school or getting another loan cosigned by someone else to stay in school, the financial aid officer explained to a sobbing Caroline Hempheart. Ultimately, she had no choice but to do something, as her classes had been dropped, and her instructors had been notified that if she showed up for class, they'd have to ask her to leave. Caroline's life was turbulent beyond belief.

Caroline was one of those students at Mason Smith University that had to load up on financial aid and student loans to afford the enormous tuition bill each year. She was well aware of the financial burden placed on her when she enrolled, as her parents had told her if they were going to pay for tuition, all they could afford was a state school, which Caroline did not find appealing.

She fussed and fought with her parents for months to go to the prestigious Mason Smith University, and finally they relented, allowing her to assume tens of thousands of dollars in student loan debt each year, without any foreseeable way to pay it back in the future.

"Hey, you want to get something to eat later?" Sandra shouted to Caroline through her door while tapping her nails on the rim of the doorknob.

"I don't know, maybe. I got to get this sociology assignment done," Caroline said to Sandra, ignoring her present circumstance for the sake of not having to explain it to her nosy roommate.

"Super, it's a plan. I'm going to Charlie's for a little bit. I'll be back around six," Sandra proclaimed as she walked away from Caroline's door.

Caroline sunk her head deep into the pillow that was now on the floor, soaking-wet, catching her still-falling tears. Becker had sensed something was wrong with Caroline, so he lay still facing her on the ground waiting for eye contact. Hours passed, and neither moved more than an inch.

Caroline's mind wandered through every possible way to get her tuition paid, or at least get a loan big enough to satisfy her debt for the semester. She just needed to make this problem go away.

Robbing a bank, holding a bake sale, and becoming a professional skier all crossed her mind. She couldn't just give up. It wasn't in her DNA to quit. She had got herself into this situation, and she was going to find a way out.

"Becker, I've got it!" Caroline said with a resounding yell as Becker leaped to his four feet.

"Where is your leash, we've got to take a trip," Caroline said to the dog now rushing to put on a pair of dark blue jeans and a button-down western shirt.

Seven snaps later, the shirt was on her body and the dog was in her arms. She kicked the door open and ran for the front door, skipping every other step for speed.

Chapter 8: Girl Power

The tight space between the lower part of the steering wheel and Caroline's abdomen cradled Becker's body as he made it his mission to watch for any intruders on either side of the car. Caroline tightened her hair with her left hand into a ponytail while the ignition was turned on with a twist of the key in her right hand. Within seconds, Caroline's car was out of her driveway and headed for the Red Beacon National Bank's regional branch in Columbus.

"You got to stay still, Becks. I have to get to this place as soon as humanly possible, OK?" Caroline rhetorically asked her dog as she inserted a burned CD of R&B star Melray, a soulful singer with a pension for singing over hip hop beats. Caroline inherited most of her music from friends that either gave her CDs or just forgot them in her house or car. The Melray CD was given to her by a friend a few months earlier in a paper jewel case with a red marker scribble of the title "Girl Power" on it.

A quick and subtle shock to her legs started Caroline enough to look at her lap. To the side of Becker sat a pink cell phone that was throbbing in vibrate mode. Caroline blindly reached for the phone while keeping her eyes on the road. In a quick flip of the handset, it was at her ear ready for conversation.

"Hello, Caroline, are you there?" a gentle male voice asked.

"Yes, Cam, thank goodness you called. You won't believe what is going on," Caroline explained, inhaling a big breathe in preparation of explaining her dire circumstances.

"I'm sorry hun, I can't stay on the phone long. The reception out here is awful. I just wanted to let you know I'll be home tonight. Sandra sent me a text message about Mexican tonight; I'll see you there." Cam responded with a click of the phone.

"Cam, are you there? Cam?" shouted a frustrated Caroline to her boyfriend that was no longer on the line.

In the background, the beat from the Melray CD started to take hold of her mind. The anger at the dropped call faded quickly, and the melody started to pulsate throughout Caroline's body. If nobody else would tell Caroline it would be OK, Melray would, and did, all the way to Columbus.

The large, black sunglasses covered her emotions enough to give Caroline the appearance of any other college-aged girl. She glanced at her face in the rearview while the music trumpeted out of the modest four speakers in her car. The proud, hardworking girl felt a rush of emotion through her veins. It was at this moment that Caroline embraced her responsibility, embraced her difference to most of her peers, and embraced her life.

Chapter 9: Doggy Meningitis

Becker's head bobbed back and forth as he ran by the side of Caroline, now in full sprint, headed for the Red Beacon National Bank building in downtown Columbus. It was 4:55 in the afternoon, and the bank closed promptly at 5:00 p.m.

In front of the bank building's large glass doors stood a moderately imposing security guard. Confused by the image of Caroline and Becker heading directly toward his bank with increasing speed, the guard simply stepped aside to let them in and shook his head.

"I'd like to speak to Peter Arnold please. Is he here?" Caroline asked the first teller that made eye contact with her, while holding the now panting Becker.

"I'm sorry, miss. There are no dogs allowed in here," responded the blank-faced teller.

"He's very sick, he could die, and I need to see Peter Arnold, now!" Caroline frantically told the teller as she started to scan the large room for Peter Arnold's office.

Peter heard a girl yelling his name, and worried that it was his own daughter, bolted out of his desk chair and pushed the glass door of his office open quickly.

"Caroline, what are you doing here?" Peter said with eyes

wide open and hands and arms unintentionally reached out.

"Hi Uncle Pete. I need to talk to you. Can we talk?" Caroline said to her shocked uncle.

"Yes, of course. Come into my office, it's OK," Peter said to Caroline as he waved off the security guard and shot the teller that had made the comment about no dogs a firm look.

"Here, sit down sweetheart," Peter said while pointing to a chair facing his large, cluttered black desk.

"What are you doing here?" Peter asked as he watched Caroline slip into the seat.

"I need a loan. Becker has meningitis and it might be fatal. I need a loan," Caroline explained to Peter.

A puzzled look crossed Peter's face as he sat and thought about what was just requested of him.

"Meningitis, dogs can get that?" Peter skeptically asked.

"Yes, they can, and we need a loan to get this dog treated. You don't want anything to happen to him, do you?" Caroline said to Peter as Becker's eyes met Peter's.

Becker looked Peter dead in the face, his little tongue hanging out of the side of his mouth, and his small black nose inhaling and exhaling in precise rhythm with his lower jaw movements. It was as close to a smile as a dog could offer, and Becker was in the moment, the game was on, and Becker was ready to play.

"You're sick, little buddy?" Peter asked rising from his office chair moving toward Becker.

Becker's tail wagged feverishly as Peter arrived to greet the young dog.

"Yes, he is sick, and without this loan, he might not live Uncle Pete. Look at this dog, you want him to live, right?" Caroline asked Peter, who was now fully engaged with Becker, petting his head and smiling at the same time.

"Have you told your Dad yet?" Peter calmly asked as he pet Becker's lower back.

"No, I haven't. I was hoping we could keep this between us," Caroline responded, not sure if she could keep this fib going much longer.

"Well I'd need to talk to your father. I could call him," Peter said while reaching out for the phone on his desk.

"No, you can't call him. It's not the dog, Uncle Pete, it's my tuition. They dropped all my classes," Caroline explained as tears started to rush from her eyes.

"What? I thought you already started school last week?" Peter asked, looking stunned.

"Yes, we started last week, but financial aid wasn't able to get all my loans approved in time. If I don't get a loan soon, I'll be forced to take the semester off," Caroline said while sobbing as she sat in the generic blue office chair.

"Hold on, let's calm down kiddo. It's not like you, or your Becker, is going to die or anything," Peter said to Caroline in an attempt to calm her down.

"Uncle Pete, if I don't get my tuition paid by Friday, I'll be forced to drop out of school for good. You and I both know I can't get back in there once this happens. I'm already so far in the hole with these loans, any time off would just seal the deal of me not going back, not finishing college," Caroline said while holding her head in her hands.

Peter felt his niece's hysteria and didn't want to see her go through any more pain. As the senior loan officer for Red Beacon National Bank's Columbus branch, his salary was one of the highest in the building. On top of the money Peter earned from his day job, he was a successful real estate investor, earning handsome payoffs for his investments in new construction apartment buildings.

"How much do you owe?" Peter asked while reaching for his checkbook.

"I am not sure, let me see," Caroline said as the tears started to dry up.

Caroline reached into her small, black purse and pulled out a hand-written note she had written earlier that day with the balance on it.

"I owe $12,238.11," Caroline recited as she grabbed Becker and placed him back on her lap.

Peter stood frozen, not sure what to do. He took a breath and wrote a check.

"Here, this is a loan from me to you. You can pay me back when you get out of school and make your first million as an actor. I'm sure you'd get cast in a movie about sick dogs," Peter said with a grin on his face, handing over the check to Caroline.

"Uncle Pete, are you sure? This is so much money, and if my dad knew, he'd be…" Caroline started to explain until Peter stopped her.

"It's OK, I know you will pay me back. We can tell your Dad once you pay me back, and he'll be proud of you for owning up to your responsibility, OK?" Peter asked as he walked over to Caroline to give her a hug.

Chapter 10: Tacos Anyone?

The walls of the popular eatery were freshly painted a reddish brown to look like Arizona dirt. Mexican Zarape blankets covered much of the walls, as did portraits of Mexican farmers at work in the fields with donkeys in tow. The establishment had a small, five-person bar near the hostess stand where five, white, college-aged kids sat and drank cheap margaritas.

To the left of the hostess stand stood a dark and dusty glass bookshelf that contained handmade folk art celebrating the popular Mexican Day of the Dead tradition. Caroline stood with her eyes fixated on one figurine that was painted to resemble a skeleton in a tuxedo. The glass shelf held the figurine in a way that made it stand out to her. She likened her situation to that of the figurine—she was dressed up and out, but she felt dead inside.

"Party of five, no smoking please," Sandra requested over Caroline's shoulder to the hostess that was overdressed in formal black pants, a white dress shirt and a black tie.

"Right this way please," the young hostess said to Caroline and Sandra, motioning them with a stack of menus to follow her to the back of the restaurant.

The hostess placed the stack of menus on a large table covered in a cheap, green plastic tablecloth.

"Enjoy your meal," the hostess said with a smile as she walked away.

"So what's up? Your eyes look all puffy. Is everything alright?" asked Sandra of Caroline, giving her a look that she knew more was going on than Caroline had mentioned that day.

"It's some tuition issues, that's all. Everything will be OK. I really just don't want to talk about it right now. Besides, Cam should be here soon. Let's just have fun tonight," Caroline pleaded to Sandra in a tone that was both somber and optimistic.

"OK girl, as long as you know I'm here for you," Sandra said to Caroline, placing her hands on the table as to conclude the serious talk for the evening.

"Hey Sandra, hey baby, how are you both doing?" Cam announced as he plopped his thick body into a wooden chair next to Caroline.

Cam's frame was anything but athletic. At a modest 5 feet 4 inches tall and 228 pounds, Caroline's boyfriend Cameron was more of a shadow of a once-fit and well-kept young man, at age 21.

As a former high school running back sensation out of the northern part of Ohio, Cameron was an exceptional athlete at his prime. After a freak accident in the gym his senior year of high school in which he hurt his left knee, Cameron called his playing days over.

Three years and 40 pounds later, Cameron still walked with a swagger of confidence, still acted like he was the big man on campus, even though most people hardly knew who he was. Caroline's friends thought she could do better, but she saw a side of Cameron they didn't. She felt one day he could change.

"I'll take a large margarita, a tall draft beer, and a shot of tequila," Cameron barked to the waitress before she could ask what everyone would want to drink.

The waitress jotted down his order without hesitation, and looked over at Caroline for hers.

"Iced tea, please, no lemon," Caroline softy said to the waitress.

"Cerveza," Sandra requested with a smile.

The waitress nodded her head in thanks, and walked away to the back of the kitchen.

"Are you thirsty, Cam?" Caroline asked her boyfriend with a smile.

"Not really, I just know the drinks here are cheap, so I figured I'd start this night off right," Cam rationalized out loud as Caroline tried to rid her face of any puzzled looks.

"It is Monday night, Caroline. You do know that, right?" Sandra said smiling, as if to signal that the week was really meant for drinking, and not thinking about serious issues like her tuition dilemma.

Caroline sat quietly while the waitress pushed her iced tea in front of her, and flipped a straw in her direction. Caroline watched as Sandra sipped her beer while trying to read the Spanish language subtitles on the television set in the corner of the restaurant.

"Are you done with that drink already, Cam?" Caroline asked with a pulse of concern as Cam plopped the empty margarita glass on the table.

"Yeah, I am done with it. It's time for another," Cam said combatively to Caroline as he licked the salt off the rim of his glass.

Caroline felt her heart rate pick up as she swigged her iced tea.

Time seemed to stand still as the three sat quietly waiting to order—Sandra gazing at the TV, Cam drinking as fast as he could, and Caroline sitting motionless, watching Cam's rotund face turn a shade of red that only alcohol could produce.

The waitress returned to the table and silently requested their order by pointing to the now evenly stacked menus sitting in front of Sandra on the table.

"I'll take another round, and three tacos," Cam ordered without hesitation.

Caroline sat silent. Was her boyfriend really going to get this drunk and not even ask what the major problem was she was having that day? Who was this guy she was dating? What in the world or who in the world did he think he was, Caroline wondered as she pointed to a combination plate of enchiladas and guacamole salad on the menu for the waitress to write down.

Sandra spoke two quick sentences in Spanish, offering up an order that neither Cam nor Caroline could decipher.

Cam started on his second round with a furry of drinking, and laughing, and slamming of glasses on the table. It seemed as quick as the waitress could bring them, Cam would toss them back.

It all started to get out of control when two of Cam's fraternity brothers came over from the bar to say hello.

"Hey Cam, you catch any big fish this weekend?" the two frat guys asked with a chuckle.

Caroline realized that Cam may not have, in fact, been fishing at all. He may have lied to her a few times in the past, and he may have lied to her a few times tonight. This was not good, but Caroline was too numb still from the tuition incident to say anything about it to him.

"You bring any dollar bills with you to the lake?" one of the two obviously inebriated frat guys asked.

"Guys shut up. Let's do a shot, OK? It's on me!" Cam said while waving over the waitress.

Within 30 seconds, three empty tequila glasses clanked against the table as the boys chanted a fraternity song that made Sandra laugh out loud.

"Omega, Phi, Sigma!" yelled one brother to another as Cam stood up, putting his arms around both of them, and guiding them back to the place they came from.

"Caroline, you got to relax, honey. You know how these guys are. They don't mean any harm by it," Sandra said to Caroline as she took inventory of Caroline's melancholy mood.

"I know Sandra, it's just that he doesn't even care about what happened today. I mean, I called him earlier and his call dropped, and I was all upset. I just figured he'd ask how I was doing, that's all," Caroline pleaded with Sandra to justify being upset at her boyfriend.

Minutes passed, as the food arrived, and Cam's chair sat empty. Sandra and Caroline ate quietly while the frat brothers took turns downing a seemingly endless amount of alcohol at the bar. Shots, beer, glasses lit on fire, nothing was off limits.

As Caroline and Sandra finally finished their dishes, Cam stumbled back to the table. His head noticeably loose, he sat down and quietly took one bite of his taco dinner.

Rather quickly, a large and bright green projectile of vomit came rushing back out of Cam's mouth like a fire hose on full blast. The contents of the vomit fell flat on Cam's full plate. He stood quietly for a minute as Sandra and Caroline looked on in horror.

"You guys want some of my tacos?" Cameron asked as he started to laugh hysterically, ignoring the disgusted guests at his table.

"That's it. I cannot take another minute of this. I'm leaving," Caroline said while standing up. She tossed a $10 bill on the table, and briskly walked out of the front door.

Chapter 11: College Road Trip

As chief reporter for the business section of the Columbus Tribune, Ryan Todd was constantly in search of the next best story to decorate the headlines of Ohio's most prestigious daily newspaper. It wasn't long ago that Ryan had been on the dead beat job of covering the smallest of small stories. Now he finally was able to cover the riveting stuff that often glossed the front page of the paper in big, bold print, with color photos and sensational headlines sure to grab any passerby's attention.

"Roland, can I have a minute of your time?" Ryan requested while peering out the large void left between his open office door and the nearest wall.

"Sure man, what's up?" Roland said with a smile, poking his head into Ryan's office.

"How many times have we run a story on local college kids involved in enterprising businesses lately?" Ryan asked with his eyes fixed on his blank yellow legal notepad.

"Not many this year. In fact, probably none at all. I'd have to check to get the exact number," Roland Smith explained back to Ryan, now also gazing at the blank yellow legal notepad.

"OK, I'm going on a college road trip. Can you ask Beth to get me a list of all college campuses within a 30-mile radius of downtown Columbus?" Ryan said to his editor as he now looked out the window.

"Sure, I'll have Beth drop that off for you ASAP. Sounds like you have a good idea with this one," Roland said while returning to his editorial desk across the newsroom.

Ryan leaped up from his desk chair, packed his notepad into a brown leather briefcase, and quickly turned for the door.

Chapter 12: Garage and Gone

With a quick push of a button from the keychain remote console in the direction of the black, glossy sports car, the doors unlocked. Tossing the briefcase in the backseat, Ryan folded into the driver's seat, pressing his 6-foot three-inch frame back on the chair to recline just enough to give his body room to stretch out.

Ryan's neck was caught and cradled by the burgundy leather headrest as he pressed two buttons on the steering wheel and a third on the dashboard.

The engine roared into gear as Ryan gently let off the clutch with his left foot while accelerating with his right. The radio auto tuned to Ryan's favorite adult alternative station, while a band whistled away a tune of loneliness and despair.

Ryan's foot depressed the gas pedal just enough to hit 50 miles per hour as the car glided onto the highway. The roof of the car slowly retracted as the car increased speed.

Ryan's eyes gazed through the crystal clear windshield as his right hand shifted gears up every few seconds prompting the car to move faster and faster. The music started to fall victim to the now heavy dose of wind coming from all directions.

A single piece of printer paper folded three times was starting to rattle under Ryan's cell phone on the passenger seat. Ryan lifted the paper from beneath the phone, and unfolded it.

"Capital University, 2.8 miles south," Ryan said out loud as his car drifted to the exit lane.

Chapter 13: Going to Sri Lanka Is So Sexy

Parked snug in between two Honda Civic sedans, Ryan flipped his door open, ignored the half-dozen students taking cell phone pictures of his car from the sidewalk, and approached the steps of Capital University's admission office.

Inside the building that resembled a courthouse more than a college administrative office, Ryan walked swiftly past generic-looking offices lit up by fluorescent bulbs. Each door displayed a single sheet of printer paper taped on the door with headings like Enrollment Services, Late Payments and Student Services. Behind the last sign, titled Campus Media, stood a lanky woman in her early 30s with dark hair in a bun and a silk blouse neatly tucked into a grey pencil skirt.

"Hello Mr. Todd. We're so glad you are here. I'm Donna Starling, the director of campus media here at Capital University," Donna Starling exclaimed in one long and perky breath.

"Hi, thanks for having me," Ryan said with a tone that accented his busy schedule for the day.

Donna Starling gripped a stack of manila folders tightly as she motioned for Ryan to sit in a rose-colored leather chair facing her desk. Ryan took off his jacket, slinging it over the back of the chair, letting the Armani woven tags sewn on the inner suit pocket show.

"So, I am interested in profiling some student businesses. Do you have any stories for me?" Ryan asked a smiling Donna Starling.

"Yes, we were able to get a few stories from our campus newspaper story archive of the last year of active students involved in their own businesses," Donna Starling explained while letting her hair drop out of the bun it had once been in.

"You are somewhat of a celebrity around this office, Mr. Todd," Donna said while a grin started to cover her face.

"I'm flattered, but really that story I did last year was just what any other journalist would do. I'm not a celebrity, just a guy that did some digging," Ryan modestly said, deflecting Donna Starling's increasing advances.

"Well, your style of writing is so vivid, and the fact that at such a young age you were able to capture such an incredible story, it was bigger than the Enron and WorldCom scandals put together, it was honestly incredible," Donna stated in a praiseworthy manner that pushed her professionalism to the side.

Donna Starling was referring to Ryan Todd's big break as a reporter—the investigative reporting that risked his life, and gained him countless industry awards, an incredible promotion and celebrity status among area journalists. It was not often a local boy produced a story with such national notoriety.

Ryan Todd had received a call from a childhood friend that the mega successful Conner Brands clothing empire, based in Columbus, Ohio, had in fact exploited child labor to new heights. Conner Brands marketed premium clothing to the fashion hungry 12- to 25-year-old demographic with sexy cuts of clothing that had never before been marketed to children, at prices that rivaled that of the most premium adult brands on the market. In short, Conner Brands was a profit-pulling machine on Wall Street, and one of the largest companies to base its operations out of Ohio.

In order to get to the bottom of the story, Ryan Todd flew to the manufacturing facilities in Sri Lanka on his own dime, took a two-month leave of absence from the Columbus Tribune, and posed as a rep from a competing clothing company interested in getting clothing manufactured at the same factory that Conner Brands utilized for a large portion of their apparel production.

In less than four weeks, Ryan Todd had discovered that not only was Conner Brands paying their factory workers less than minimum wage in Sri Lanka, it was in fact inflating its labor costs at home to fatten the pockets of the CEO.

The story had all the trappings of national headline material. There was the greedy CEO manipulating children for $20 million bonuses, or the part about the children being paid so little they had to walk home barefoot because they could not afford shoes, while at the same time producing shorts that would sell for upwards of $100 a pair in the U.S.

Adding to the sensational nature of story was the physical altercation Ryan Todd got into with the CEO of Conner Brands on his return. The CEO, Ken Smith, when confronted by Ryan Todd in the parking lot of the massive Conner Brands corporate headquarters about the allegations of corruption in the company, attempted to strangle Ryan Todd after a short exchange of words, leaving Ryan with a bloody lip, bruise marks on his neck, and a front-page picture that would forever change his life. Ryan was able to free himself from the confrontation, rush to his car, and take as many digital pictures of his face as he could before the paramedics arrived to clean him up.

"Are you married, Mr. Todd?" asked Donna Starling with a straight face that implied interest and immediacy in his response.

"No, I'm not married, and you can call me, Ryan," Ryan answered, thumbing through the folders of archived stories about small businesses started by students at Capital University.

"What about this one—the Internet business that offers $20 dorm cleaning. Are these students still around?" Ryan asked quickly without looking up.

"Yes, they are still around. Do you want me to run their class schedule through the computer and see if we can grab them for an interview?" Donna asked.

"Please, go ahead and see if they can come down here within the next half hour or so. I'd like to talk to them," Ryan requested while pulling out his Blackberry from the holster clipped onto his belt.

"I'll be right back, Mr. Todd, I mean Ryan," Donna Starling said with a smile as she exited the room.

Ryan's face turned from pensive to sad. The emptiness inside him was knocking and he had no choice but to open the door.

Chapter 14: Ice Cold Shower

Three tall men stood hovering over an old wooden bed with large buckets of ice in hand. One man quietly counted off five seconds, and in unison they all emptied their buckets onto a half-naked body passed out asleep on the bed.

"What the hell are you doing?" Cameron yelped as he leaped from his bed to the floor, revealing his vintage teddy bear boxer shorts.

"Hahahaha, good morning brother," one of the three men shouted as he hysterically laughed at the now dripping wet Cameron.

After an initial eruption of laughter from the perpetrators of the prank, silence started to take over the room. The four individuals stood in silence for several seconds before Cameron's face started to grin from ear to ear as he grappled one of the three fraternity brothers to the ground, causing the half-empty bucket of ice laying on the floor to flip up in the air and empty out its remaining contents.

"You guys have something coming back to you, that is all I can say right now," Cameron jovially said as he wrestled his way back to his bed.

"Now get the hell out of here, I've got class to sleep through,"

Cameron noted as his three fraternity brothers started to shift for the door.

When the room had cleared, Cameron looked down at his jeans and saw the number 878-4142 written in blue pen on the pant leg of his jeans.

878 was a campus extension that was reserved for students that lived in the old brick dormitories at Mason Smith University. The number didn't resonate with Cameron—most of his friends either lived off campus or in the fraternity house where he lived.

A minute passed before Cameron realized that the mystery phone number staring him in the face was in fact jotted down by a girl he had met the night before at a mixer party held by his fraternity.

Flashes of the night crept back into Cameron's mind. There was the grain alcohol punch that he drank in excess of 32 ounces at a time. And the music, the pulsating Latin salsa rhythms played by the DJ in a sequence that made the songs seem like they never ended.

The young blonde girl hadn't been in college more than two months and she seemed to cling to Cameron. The dancing was hot, the kissing even hotter. Cameron seemed to indulge in the girl's ignorance. The less she knew about a fraternity guy like him, the better.

What was her name, Cameron wondered as he rolled his head from one side of the pillow to the other. Did he sleep with her, Cameron wondered, as it wouldn't have been the first girl he had slept with this week that wasn't his girlfriend.

It wasn't more than a minute before the soaking-wet Cameron was in dry clothing walking out the door with phone in hand, dialing the number on his pant leg.

Chapter 15: The Queen of Financial Aid

"You are good to go sweetheart. Your professors will get an e-mail this morning letting them know its OK to let you back into class," The financial aid officer explained to Caroline as she handed over the check her uncle had given her the day before.

"Thanks Mrs. Priester, I really appreciate this," Caroline said with a sincere tone of gratitude that made the other financial aid officers take notice of her presence.

Caroline turned and headed for the door of the generic office suite housed in an old house on campus. Grey felt cubicle walls kept the seven staff members of the office tucked away out of sight of those students that came through the thick wooden door for appointments.

"Caroline, I wanted to tell you something," explained a financial aid officer from the left side of the room, standing up to her feet and tilting her neck back enough to meet Caroline's eyes over the cubicle wall.

"You are really taking on a lot of debt, and I know your parents don't have much, but I wanted to tell you that you are very brave and courageous for staying in school here," the officer exclaimed as Caroline's eyes started to water.

"You will find a way to get this all paid off when you graduate school, I know you will," said another person from the other side of the room, as Caroline's eyes scanned over the room in search of the new voice.

"Thanks, I really enjoy this school, and just thank you all for working with me through these financial issues that I have been having," Caroline explained to a now captivated crowd of financial aid loan officers and administrators.

Caroline felt embarrassed that her financial issues were such public discourse in this office, but felt safe enough behind the heavy door of the office to open up and take the praise.

Caroline's finances, or lack there of had been common knowledge around the financial aid office. The small enrollment of just 1,800 students at Mason Smith University made each one more than a name and a case number. The few that needed financial aid were looked after like precious assets. Each case that the office would handle was taken very seriously, and often discussed in groups of officers to help find the most advantageous aid package for each individual student. Mason Smith University prided itself on having the best financial aid resources in the nation.

Caroline's case was an anomaly in many ways. There was the fact that her parents weren't poor in a traditional sense. The income levels of both parents were rather high, and it was simply the past debt from several bad real estate deals that left them with little money to spend on Caroline's tuition. There was the fact that Caroline's grades were above average, but not good enough to land her any prestigious scholarships that would be able to cover the massive tuition fees each year. And most notably, Caroline's affable personality and genuine affection for the university pulled at the heartstrings of all those in the office that knew her, or at least had heard about her case.

Caroline walked through the door, pushing with both hands at the last minute to swing it open. Once in the staircase, Caroline felt a tear threatening to drop from her eye, as she wiped it away with her sleeve and told herself there was no time for tears, she had a sociology class to attend.

Chapter 16: GoodTube Sucks

Making her way up the steps of the John T. Rogers Center for Sociological Studies building where she had her sociology class starting in two minutes, Caroline felt a tap on her shoulder.

"What the hell is this?" Cameron asked, pointing to his sleek, black cell phone that had a tiny video playing on its screen mixed with whisper-level shouts that sounded like static to Caroline.

The video showed Caroline, four years earlier shedding her top in front of a crowd of a dozen people that had been chanting, "Flash, flash, flash." The party took place while Caroline was in high school near the end of her career, and half of the girls in the video had shed their tops, just not when someone had been filming.

A GoodTube logo covered the right corner of the screen, giving Caroline the notification that it wasn't just Cameron that had seen this video. GoodTube was the largest online video Web site in the world, with millions of visitors every hour watching videos just like this one. Caroline was mortified.

Cameron pushed the phone closer to Caroline's face until it was just inches from her eyes. A single tear drop broke the silence between them by falling on the tiny cell phone screen.

"You stripper, you hooker, you prostitute. I don't date prostitutes,"

Cameron yelled at a still Caroline.

"That, Cam, that is not me," Caroline muttered while her lower jaw started to tremble.

"I mean it's me, but it's not me anymore. I hardly ever go out, you are the one that…" Caroline began to say before a passerby shouted at them both.

"Sex tape drama!" a random guy said while he chuckled his way past the two of them.

"It's not a sex tape, Cameron. It's a stupid, 17-year-old girl that was a few months from graduation acting silly," Caroline pleaded to a red-faced Cameron.

"My friends pointed this video out to me. They've all seen it. They all think I'm with some kind of cheap hooker," Cameron said, letting his eyes wander over Caroline's shoulder to a girl walking up the steps in a short skirt.

"Look, it's over, OK? It is o-v-e-r," Cameron said as he turned his back on Caroline and walked away.

Caroline stood motionless, not sure whether to be upset about the horrid video, or the fact that Cameron would actually break up with her for such a thing. Who filmed it? Who posted it? Caroline's mind raced.

A wave of emotion pounded through Caroline's heart, and made itself known with the pulsating beats that increased beyond Caroline's control. Her eyes were overflowing with tears of embarrassment and frustration. Her hands were shaking uncontrollably.

Caroline pushed herself forward, up the steps gripping the brass door handle of the building, swinging it open, and forcing herself to walk through the door.

Caroline walked into a silent classroom full of students watching her find a seat. The professor paused her lecture while he saw a crying Caroline fumble from seat to seat. Noticing her emotions, the professor acted quickly.

"Let's all have a look at this diagram on the board," Professor Katie Reynolds said, picking up a piece of chalk that hadn't been touched in two years.

"I am going to show you all how a nuclear family would look if they were each represented by one of these lines," Professor Reynolds said while feverishly drawing four long lines and one short line on the chalk board.

The professor hadn't touched the board since she started teaching at the university two years prior. She had a secret irritation to the sound of chalk on the board, and many of the students were catching on to the distraction technique.

"Mrs. Reynolds, we haven't talked about the nuclear family in four weeks. Is this diagram somehow connected to our current reading on the digital divide?" asked one of the better students in the class.

"Yes, we can only understand the dynamics of this current lesson by looking at our past model of a nuclear family," the professor rattled off, looking the student in the eye so as to let the student know she was not kidding around.

Caroline's tears, as hard as she tried, could not stop coming. Caroline realized her teacher's kind effort to take the attention away from her, which in turn made her reflect on her financial problems and the struggle to stay in school for teachers like Professor Reynolds.

An older man sitting behind Caroline tossed his old sweatshirt on her lap and whispered something to her.

Caroline took the sweatshirt, buried her face in it, and let it all out.

Chapter 17: Hyenas

Caroline sat quietly in her car. She wanted to call someone and tell them what happened, but she realized if she did, they'd have that video up on their computers, mobile phones or whatever other gadget they had handy that connects to the Internet.

How did this happen, Caroline kept asking herself. She knew Cameron wasn't perfect, but she dearly cared about him. She saw herself marrying that man, and starting a family, regardless of how many people had told her she could do better.

Caroline's mind rationed the thoughts in delicate compartments. There were the thoughts about how she could have been so loyal to such a jerk like Cameron, which got placed into the loyal and dumb compartment. Another area of her brain muddled over thoughts of how people could carelessly and often without thought for what they were doing or who they were hurting post videos like the one of Caroline on the Internet. The final and furthest compartment catching thoughts in Caroline's mind was the security area of her brain. She entertained thoughts of a life without issue, a life of privilege, a life of making money not debt, and having a family that appreciated her rise from the struggle that was her life. That distant compartment helped push Caroline to move forward with her life.

Caroline's hands shook as she thought of all the people that would see her half naked on the Internet. She felt compromised, she felt cheapened, and most notably, she felt angry. Caroline had deliberately stayed far away from most of the temptations of college. While she hadn't forbid drinking, she hardly engaged in it. While she hadn't forbid hanging out with large groups of friends, she never made it a priority to do that either.

Caroline was, by most people's standards, a loner. She had a few friends, and most of them were from circumstance—her uncle had to be her friend because he was her uncle, Sandra had to be her friend because she was her roommate. Caroline didn't give herself the credit to have made friends without a circumstance that dictated that kind of relationship.

A piercing pain went down Caroline's spine as a memory came to her mind. Caroline didn't want to go there, but she did anyway.

Just a month earlier, Caroline and Sandra and two of Sandra's girlfriends stood huddled around a laptop computer screen while they laughed hysterically at a student from Mason Smith University shown wandering around a party in a series of drunken movements. The video had been edited to highlight each of the most outrageous things the student said and did that night. Caroline pictured a crow picking at the bones of a helpless body of a dead dog, while the hyenas cackled in the background. She felt awful.

Disgusted at her past behavior and furious with her current situation, Caroline opened her eyes and sat up straight in her car seat.

"That's it, I am done with it," Caroline sternly announced, her eyes staring back at her in the rearview mirror as she tossed her cell phone out her car window.

Chapter 18: Dry Cleaned Jeans

Two young men sat in old wooden desk chairs facing Ryan Todd with smiles on their faces as they took turns answering his questions. The rapid-fire question and answer session had been moving along nicely for a half hour, and the young men seemed to revel in the interest from the Tribune reporter.

"So you guys clean anything for 20 bucks?" Ryan asked with a raised eyebrow.

"Yes, beer cans, mayo, chips, dirty clothes, you name it. If it is in a dorm room, we clean it," the taller man responded with a smile.

"The boys have been very busy with business this semester. Their idea really works well on this campus," said Donna Starling with a smile while nodding at the two young men.

Ryan feverishly took notes, asking several questions that needed clarification from Donna Starling before the two young men could answer.

"How long have you turned a profit? What's your gross looking like this year, and how's your net shaping up?" Ryan Todd rattled off, scanning the boy's young faces for answers.

"Are you turning a profit or just breaking even?" Donna Starling asked as if to interpret Ryan Todd's latest question.

"Well, we were able to buy a flat screen TV for our own room last week. It took a few months of doing this, but it's pretty sweet," explained one of the young men with a blank expression that gave away the fact he really didn't know much about finance.

"So let me ask you two more questions," Ryan said with a grin, which helped Donna Starling smile even wider than she already had been.

"You guys clean a lot of rooms. What is the most bizarre thing you found when cleaning a room?" Ryan Todd asked, bracing for the answer.

"We found a dead raccoon in one girl's room last semester," the taller student answered with a smile.

"Yeah, she called us and asked us to help clean her room to get rid of a strong smell that she couldn't seem to find the source of," the other student answered.

"Turns out it was her ex-boyfriend that had planted a dead raccoon in her room. He was trying to get even with her for cheating on him or something. All I know is that was one stinky coon," the taller student explained.

Ryan Todd sat quietly. Not sure whether to laugh or get sick, he moved on to his next question.

"So what is the most surprising thing about this business so far?" Ryan Todd asked while flipped the pages of his legal pad to the front, indicating he was about finished with the interview.

"How many guys have really clean rooms," the student answered.

"Yeah, some of these guys have these impeccable rooms with like perfectly folded sheets, carpets that have been steam cleaned, dry cleaned jeans. You'd never think college guys would be into all that," the taller student explained.

Chapter 19: Columbus Chill

The BMW's engine roared into gear as Ryan Todd sped away from the sparse campus. His notes crinkled around the steering wheel while he turned it gently from side to side. A brisk Ohio breeze reminded Ryan that it was indeed fall as his convertible top started to close above his head.

"Hello, talk to me," Ryan spoke into the handset of his cell phone as he flipped it open and placed it close to his ear.

"Hi Ryan, it's Beth. I have your next appointment if you are ready for it," the editorial secretary from the Columbus Tribune said in a pleasant voice.

"Perfect. I'm sure it can't beat my last interview, but we can try," Ryan said sarcastically as he switched lanes on the large highway that circled around Columbus.

"I've got you set up at Mason Smith University for a two o'clock appointment with the student affairs director, Bernard Richardson. Do you know how to get there from where you are?" Beth asked with a genuine concern that showed both a willingness to help and a respectfulness to let Ryan find his own way at the same time.

"Yes, I'll find it, thanks," Ryan said quickly as he glanced at his watch reading a quarter till two in the afternoon.

Chapter 20: Internet Boycott

"Bernard Richardson, director of student affairs. Are you OK?" Bernard said with an extended hand to a sobbing Caroline as she entered his office.

Caroline stood at the foot of the door, awkwardly shaking the man's hand while trying to cease the steady flow of tears coming from her eyes.

Caroline's tall and slender frame was wrapped in a black sundress with matching black flip flops, an outfit so casual Bernard Richardson instantly pegged her as a student. Caroline's long black hair lay flat a full eight inches beneath her broad shoulders. Her skin tanned from her daily jogs in the park and her arms lean and showcased by the cut of the dress made Bernard Richardson take notice immediately of this upset student in his office.

"Nice to meet you, Caroline. What can I help you with today?" Bernard asked, ignoring the fact that she had been crying just seconds prior, the tears still noticeably hanging on her thin cheeks.

"I'd like to inform you I will no longer be using computers on or off campus for my classes," Caroline said with a straight face as if she were issuing an arrest warrant to a criminal.

"I'm sorry, what?" Bernard asked as if he had needed her to explain this foreign concept another time for his mind to get a grip on it.

"I'm boycotting computers all together. I think they are awful. Not just computers—I'm actually not using a cell phone, Ipod or any other computer-type gadget that can connect to the Internet," Caroline said, giving away the fact that she didn't know much of the technological descriptions for her devices.

"I see. Well, if you can't afford a computer, the library has plenty for our students to use," Bernard shot off with an answer so stock it came directly from the university handbook.

"I do not think you understand, Mr. Richardson. I am no longer using the Internet or anything that involves the Internet. Can I still feasibly pass my classes? Is it possible?" Caroline shouted as her frustration mounted, realizing there was no going back from this declaration of Internet independence.

"Well I suppose so. I mean, you'd have to talk with your teachers, but as far as the university rules go, you should be OK," Bernard explained with a gentle smile, hoping to calm the upset student down enough to bring back her indoor voice.

Two knocks broke the conversation as Ryan Todd pushed the office door open six inches and stuck his head in the doorway. Caroline turned around, thinking it was a school administrator that had heard her shouting and was checking to see what the screaming was all about.

"Everything is OK, You can go back to work now," Caroline said without thinking.

"I don't work here," Ryan responded without hesitation.

Caroline watched as Ryan walked into the room. His tall frame bobbing under the doorway to enter, his suit impeccably fit to his body, strutting forward with a demeanor that matched his appearance. Ryan's short, dark hair remained perfectly unkept as he moved toward Caroline.

Caroline's eyes gave away her interest immediately. Ryan's heart started to beat faster, and his throat tightened to a point where words could barely come out of it.

"Is everything OK in here? I just heard something outside," Ryan said with a higher than normal tone that gave away his nervousness.

"I'm Bernard Richardson," Bernard said while extending his hand to Ryan's outstretched hand. After shaking briefly, the three stood in silence. Richardson, shocked from the bizarre Internet outrage he'd never seen before and unsure whether to comfort the student or write an academic paper on it, stood still.

Ryan's eyes remained transfixed on Caroline's slender body. He'd never seen anyone like her in his life. She was sophisticated beyond the typical college student; Ryan hoped she was his age, and that she'd heard of him. He was dying to impress her.

"I'm Ryan Todd. I work for the Columbus Tribune," Ryan explained, keeping his eyes fixed on Caroline's gentle face.

"OK, and you are here for the Internet boycott?" Bernard Richardson asked with a perplexed look on his face.

"Yes, he is here to do a story on it, and if you don't let me finish classes because I refuse to use a computer it could be some bad press for your university," Caroline said, breaking her staring match with Ryan to look at a now puzzled Bernard.

"I never said you couldn't finish classes, I just said you should talk to your teachers," Bernard explained with a quick glance at the clock hanging above his office door.

Ryan stood speechless, watching Caroline as she spoke to Bernard Richardson, pleading her case and explaining how upset she was with technology as a whole.

"I'd need to do an interview with you," Ryan said to Caroline, who had now risen from her chair and turned to come face to face with Ryan.

Inches apart, they stood looking at each other as Bernard Richardson sat at his desk looking up at the two of them with utter confusion.

"Interviews are fine with me. Just make sure you turn your gadgets off," Caroline said to Ryan as she moved for the door, pointing to the Blackberry cell phone tandem held in dual holsters on his belt.

Chapter 21: Net Offensive

Pictures of past university presidents and officials hung from the walls of the small conference room in the student affairs office. Two wooden seats covered in red felt cushions with worn tiny dots of decaying felt hanging off the sides of the chairs sat empty facing each other as Ryan Todd and Caroline Hempheart stood face to face near the door.

"Did you want to sit down?" Ryan asked Caroline softly to assure her he was one of the good guys.

"No I am OK, We can just stand," Caroline said with defiance, not sure whether to be excited or embarrassed by the happenings of the afternoon.

"OK, we can just stand here, I just wanted to get a few questions answered for this story that I am apparently doing on you," Ryan said with a chuckle.

"Alright, that will be fine," Caroline said, trying not to show her excitement toward the young reporter.

Ryan thumbed through his notebook trying to think of something clever to say.

"How long do you plan to boycott the Internet?" Ryan asked while clicking his pen into writing form.

"The rest of the school year," Caroline responded without

hesitation.

Caroline could feel her palms moisten from the nerves that danced inside her. She was liberated from what she felt was a major culprit of her own problems, and in turn standing next to one of the most handsome men she had ever seen. She'd never seen anyone like Ryan before. Tall but not lanky, friendly but not overtly so, and most importantly well spoken, but not to the point of being arrogant, he was in her mind a lovely soul.

Ryan spoke softly, asking her question after question about her plight, but all the while smiling and reassuring her of his position that her cause was a noble one. Caroline stood answering each question, all the while wondering how long she'd have to go before she could hold him in her arms, she felt compelled to inquire.

"When will I be getting a hug?" Caroline asked as if it were something that took place for all his interviewees.

"I was unaware you were waiting for one. Would you like one now?" Ryan asked, breaking his cadence of reporter talk just long enough to respond to Caroline's inquiry.

Caroline took two steps forward with her arms extended, and pushed forward into his arms. She held him tightly as he held her loosely at first, and then tightened his grip as hers did the same.

Ryan wondered if she'd cry again, but she didn't. She just kept still in his arms for what seemed like minutes. Ryan closed his eyes and rested his head against hers as he smelled the kind scent of Caroline's herbal shampoo, a scent he'd never smelled before.

"It's eucalyptus mango berry, if you must know," Caroline remarked, catching Ryan off guard enough for him to let out a small laugh.

Caroline did not want to let go of Ryan. Although she had just met him, he felt secure to her, in a world that was anything but.

A clank of the door knob into the nearby wall startled the two away from each other as Bernard Richardson walked in.

"Sharing a protesters moment, eh?" Bernard Richardson said with a grin.

The two smiled. They'd been busted by the school official, something that gave Ryan a rush of excitement he hadn't felt in a long time.

"C'mon, you two, it's time to get out of here. I'm taking lunch and locking this place up behind me," Bernard Richardson said with a sigh as he flipped the light switch of the conference room to the off position.

Chapter 22: Say Something Stupid

The Ohio chill greeted Ryan and Caroline with a windy gust as the two opened the double doors simultaneously and exited the building with a brisk trio of steps. They stood motionless facing each other as the doors closed behind them.

Green trees signaled the direction of the wind with branches humped over allowing groups of leaves to blow. The blades of grass shined a color of green so lush it looked artificial. Blossoming flowers in large numbers sat in a bed of soil surrounding the outside of the building. Students walked through the startling picture of nature with little regard for it, talking on their cell phones, fiddling with their iPods, and chatting with one another as they passed Ryan and Caroline standing on the concrete steps.

Caroline's dress pushed back on her body by the wind gave Ryan new insight into her figure. Her beauty inside was rivaled only by her athletic figure that could've graced any fashion magazine cover in the world, Ryan thought. Her face was soft and remarkably well kept for a college student. It was the epitome of beauty in Ryan's mind, a shape and texture he'd only seen abroad. He wondered if Caroline had been born in an exotic far away country, maybe entering the U.S. at a young enough age to adapt to the language as if she were born here. He stopped wondering in an instant. A flash of him saying something stupid and ruining the moment came to his mind, bringing him down to earth for the first time in more than an hour.

"I've got to go to my next appointment. I mean, my next interview downtown at Ohio State," Ryan said awkwardly, trying to keep his fear of saying something stupid hidden.

"I'll call you later. What's your number?" Ryan said before Caroline could respond to his initial comment.

"I don't have one, remember? I'm giving up cell phones," Caroline said with a sincere smile as her hair began to pick up from the wind.

"OK, well how can I get in touch with you?" Ryan asked while gazing into Caroline's eyes one last time, an indulgence he couldn't seem to stop doing.

"You'll just have to find me. I'll be around," Caroline said with an immediate feeling of regret.

Ryan smiled and walked away from Caroline, quickly moving down the steps of the building toward his car. His mind raced. Was he mislead? Did she not feel like he did? They were questions that would linger in his mind forever if they couldn't be answered by her. He wanted to turn around, but he didn't. The risk of saying something stupid and ruining the moment was too real, too impending for him to have dared say a word. He vowed not to look back, and as bad as he wanted to see her one last time, he kept walking.

Caroline stood watching Ryan walk away, upset at her remark, knowing she wanted to see him just as badly as he wanted to see her, but she didn't know what else to say. She rationalized it was best to keep it casual. She was in no place to get attached. She still felt livid at Cam and needed time to heal; at least that is what she thought she needed.

Chapter 23: Roasted Peanut Aroma

A day-old bag of roasted peanuts sat four feet above the floor on an old end table and let off a scent that begged Becker to reach it. The small, white dog sat at the foot of the table, every few seconds springing its small rear legs off the floor in an effort to summit the table. Becker's small, furry head arched back as he leapt in the air to get a glimpse of the mystery scent, while his front two paws attempted to knock it to the floor. Just a few more inches and Becker would've had those peanuts; it was just out of reach for the young dog.

After countless attempts at obtaining the nuts, Becker took a break on the old brown beanbag chair in the corner of Caroline's room. Effortlessly jumping onto the beanbag, Becker surveyed the room for humans. None were present.

The dog sat quietly, resting it's head on two extended paws while at the same time stretching out his two rear paws to obtain maximum comfort. The dog's body lay motionless while his two eyes scanned the room for life. The roasted peanuts seemed to catch the hazel eyes of Becker as he scanned the room from end to end.

A faint ring came from across the hall, the sound penetrating the closed door of Caroline's small room. Becker rose, leaping off the beanbag chair and toward the door. Determined to defend the space from whatever enemy would make such a sound, Becker stood a foot from the door waiting for something to happen.

After several more rings, it stopped. Becker continued to stand at the door, tail wagging, waiting for his owner to return, possibly with some tool or device to help bring the roasted peanuts to the floor.

Chapter 24: Typeface

"You want to do what? I don't think so, not in my classroom," Arnold Sawyer, the old and rigid Asian history professor pronounced to Caroline with a royal "don't question my authority" tone that sank Caroline's body deeper into her seat.

"But Dr. Sawyer, if you just knew what technology is doing to young adults these days. I mean, it's a travesty," Caroline explained to the professor that kept a freshly appalled look on his face for effect.

"Look, Caroline, it's not that I don't think the Internet has spun things out of control, because I think it has. Look at any recent disaster and the Internet played a part in it. Everything from 9/11 to the Virginia Tech shootings, the Internet had some role in facilitating these tragedies. The terrorists used the Internet to plot, recruit, and eventually plan out the 9/11 attack. And the shooter from Virginia Tech, he used the Internet to purchase the bullets that were used that day. It's despicable, I understand that. However, I just can't let you handwrite all your assignments. it's impossible since we require students to electronically submit their papers via the Internet so the graduate assistants across campus can log in and grade the papers. Your handwritten papers just will not work for us," Professor Sawyer explained while looking Caroline over for understanding.

Caroline sat quietly for several seconds, plotting her rebuttal. She knew the professor was as wise as his old age implied, but she knew she had a case for consideration, and since he wasn't a law professor, she reasoned having some legal grounding to help back up her argument would work best.

"Professor Sawyer, if you think I am saying I don't like the Internet, you are wrong. I understand it offers good and bad, and the good probably does outweigh the bad. However, I have a personal issue with what the Internet has done to my privacy. I am saying it is a breach of my privacy for me to use it, and therefore I am asking, or legally telling you that I am going to handwrite my papers. There is no information anywhere on any campus-approved materials forcing students to use computers for classes. If you failed me, you would in effect be discriminating against my right to choose how I complete my assignments," Caroline sternly said as the adrenaline rushed through her veins.

"Can you at least type it and print it out?" the professor said with a sigh.

"Well, I could use a typewriter, if I can find one," Caroline said with a smile.

"OK, go find one, and please, give this whole no Internet thing some thought," Professor Sawyer said as he pushed his chair out from his desk, stood up, and headed for the classroom door.

Chapter 25: Incomplete

Ryan sat quietly at his office desk looking for a reason to go looking for the girl he had met the day before. Caroline's dress pushing up against her perfect frame in the wind kept entering Ryan's mind. The image would start with Ryan gazing at Caroline's feet, and then slowly his eyes would move up her body until their eyes met. He could feel Caroline's energy for him, he could see her reciprocating every feeling he was putting out into the universe for her, and it drove him wild. The visualization, however, was bittersweet for Ryan, as he was unsure he'd ever see her again.

Gentle rays from the moon pinstriped Ryan's large office as the quiet, melodic tone of desktop computers sitting idle muffled by cubicle walls ran through the area. The compuorchestra kept Ryan's mind reflecting on his seemingly perfect life being anything but. His mind, his heart, his soul begged for company, for guidance, for a life outside of the one it was living in.

Ryan's eyes rolled from side to side as his mind raced. There had to be a way to see her again he thought, as he rested his shoulders on his otherwise empty office desk.

Pushing his chair out from the desk, Ryan rolled toward the window of his office, the wheels of his chair catching on his laptop power cord. Ryan quickly stood up, as he realized the answer to his problems had just stopped him in his tracks.

Chapter 26: Droll Blotter

The rowdy students exchanged words as if they were about to enter an underground cave that would make them all deaf in the next minute. As the class swelled with students looking for desks and plopping overstuffed book bags on chairs to mark their territory, Caroline slowly made her way to the back of the classroom.

"Hey flasher, how they hanging today?" remarked a burly, scruffy boy sitting to the left of Caroline's freshly chosen desk.

"Hi, we're all still here," Caroline quipped, not knowing what she meant by the statement and not caring what the person next to her really thought about her anyways.

The boy sat still, gazing at Caroline as the rest of the class shuffled their notebooks from their bags to the desks as the professor made an inaudible request to visit chapter 10 for test review.

The classroom seated 20 comfortably, but nearly 30 were in the room cramming for the big quarterly exam that was fast approaching. Some stood against the wall while others shared a desk chair, all facing the front of the classroom trying to find the knowledge needed to at least pass the upcoming test.

Caroline flipped her notebook open to a blank page, clicked her pen to the writing position, and immediately started to space out.

Her mind drifted far from academics to all the places that had emotionally touched her in the past several days. She thought about her uncle and his generosity to keep her in school. She kept thinking about how she wanted to not only repay him, but one day gives him his own bank to run, once she had made her first million.

Caroline's left foot began to flex up and down allowing her flip flop to tap against her heel like a rubber ball on a string connected to a paddle. Her foot flexed in greater veracity as she thought about Cameron.

The image of Cameron on the steps calling her those names made her furious. Her face turned red, her heart started to race, and she turned to the boy next to her and tapped him on the shoulder.

"You look like an unmade bed, I'm sure you've never had a girlfriend, and you're probably going to keep that streak alive for many years to come. Your false confidence makes me sick, your appearance makes me ill, and your attitude makes me want to toss up my lunch," Caroline said loud enough for half the room to hear.

Caroline's eyes remained fixed on the boy after the remarks left her mouth. She wanted to watch the castle of confidence crumble, and with each wince from the boy's face, Caroline's own confidence grew. She knew she was in control, and it invigorated her.

Taking her eyes away from the boy's embarrassment, Caroline began to refocus on the front of the classroom, the boring lecture, and her space out on pause. She mentally pressed play and began to daydream again.

Reflecting back on the meeting with the student affairs official made Caroline's blood pressure rise again. Thinking of his condescending looks and genuine confusion of her plight made her blood boil. How could he not understand, she thought as she felt her foot clapping the rubber sole of her flip flop again.

Before she could think another thought, an image of Ryan's charming face popped into her mind. The memory of his sweet and subtle voice made her dizzy with excitement. He was a real person, a nice person, an understanding person, Caroline thought as she felt her mouth dry up.

Palms sweating, Caroline imagined Ryan's hands holding hers as he whispered in her ear how much he loved her, how much he wanted to take care of her, to be there for her, to be one with her.

"That's it, class. See you Monday for the test," the professor shouted as students rose from their chairs as quick as soldiers saluting a commander. Caroline stood up quickly, grabbed her bag while patting her face with the sleeve of her shirt for any drool as she headed for the door.

Walking out the door and quickly down the hallway, Caroline approached a corner, turned it with speed, and walked right into a tall man in a suit.

"I'm so sorry, I wasn't looking," Caroline said while gaining her balance and picking up her bag off the floor.

"It's OK, I was actually hoping I'd bump into you," Ryan said with a smile as he tried to keep his heart rate under a million beats per second.

"Ryan, what are you doing here? I'm so happy to see…" Caroline started to say as Ryan grabbed her arm.

"I need to know if we can…" Ryan started to ask as Caroline

covered his mouth with her long, thin hands.

"Yes, let's go. I need to get a typewriter so we should go together," Caroline said while giving Ryan a look that indicated she had the power to read minds.

"Oh, that's great, I love typewriters," Ryan said without thinking.

"I need one for class, and you have a car, and you are in the typing industry, so I figure you can help me find one," Caroline said with a smile, walking past Ryan toward the door hoping with all her heart he'd follow.

"Sure, I'm a closet pawn shop junkie, so I can take you on a pawn shop tour and see if we can't find you a typewriter. Plus I wanted to get some questions answered for the article I'm doing on you," Ryan said while trying to catch up to Caroline's stride as they both dodged students coming in and out of the building.

"I'll answer any question you want me to, Ryan, any question under the sun," Caroline said as she confidently walked toward Ryan's BMW.

Chapter 27: Breathe Deep

We look like a power couple, like JFK and Jackie O or Will Smith and Jada Pinkett. That's what we look like, a total power couple, Ryan thought as his car purred in idle at a stoplight in downtown Columbus.

Caroline inhaled and exhaled deep breaths as she tried to stay calm. A vision of two dozen butterflies ravishing a single dandy lion in her stomach kept entering into Caroline's mind. She was so nervous, yet she was at the same time so excited, it was hard to keep it all in. Deep breathing, her high school swim coach told her, was the key to calming down and not getting so excited the body couldn't perform.

"Here is a good pawn shop up ahead. Do you want to check it out?" Ryan asked, looking at Caroline in mid-breath.

"Yes, let's go there and see what they have," Caroline said quietly.

"OK, well if you can break off that Lamaze session for a few minutes, that sounds like a plan," Ryan said with a grin.

Caroline laughed out loud as she looked at Ryan smiling, his suit still crisp from the dry cleaners, his tie adjusted to the side of his collar just enough to tell people he was off work for the day.

With a gentle tap on the brake pedal, the car came to a stop in a parking spot directly in front of the pawn shop. Ryan flipped his door open and walked to the passenger side to open Caroline's door. She gently folded out of the car and onto the sidewalk as he gripped two quarters out of his pocket and fed the meter's insatiable coin appetite.

The two walked side by side toward the door of the pawn shop. Ryan sped up enough to open the door for Caroline as she walked into the store.

Chapter 28: Typewriter Heaven

"We ain't got no Viagra, no purple pills, no big screen projection TV sets, and no shotguns. Other than that, how can I help ya?" the man behind the checkout counter remarked with a tone that was neither serious nor humorous.

"We're looking for a typewriter. You have any of those?" Ryan asked, unphased by the clerk's greeting.

Caroline stood behind Ryan speechless.

"No, we only have computers. We have some great computers though," the clerk said, walking around the counter in an effort to guide the two toward the used computers aisle of the store.

"We need a typewriter, so I guess we'll be on our way," Ryan said while he laced his fingers in-between Caroline's and gripped her hand tight enough to lead her to the door.

Ryan smiled as he felt her soft hands hold his tightly. He never knew holding hands could feel so good. The cold relationships Ryan had in the past never afforded him any feelings like this one. Who knew a simple holding of hands could feel like heaven, Ryan thought as they walked out of the store together.

"Let's try that pawn shop on Columbus Avenue—the one with all those old trumpets in the window. I think they are an antique shop/pawn shop," Caroline remarked as Ryan opened her car door for her.

"OK, I think I know where that is. I'm sure they will have one," Ryan said, although unsure as he had ever been if typewriters were still available anywhere in Columbus, nonetheless the next shop they were headed to.

"So what does this button do?" Caroline playfully asked while she depressed the large black knob situated in the middle of the dashboard just above the radio with her index finger, holding it down for several seconds for effect.

"It makes the world a more beautiful place," Ryan responded, evidently stoked by Caroline's curious fingers caressing his beast of an automobile.

Five steel frames folded into one another as the roof tucked itself away into the trunk of the car, allowing the sun to fill the car with a glistening of midday warmth.

Ryan, feeling the sun arrive on his face, pushed the pedal of his car toward the floor as the wind started to pick up Caroline's hair.

The car turned onto Columbus Avenue and a series of eight stoplights perfectly aligned above the center of each crossroad shined a green light in unison, giving Ryan a supernatural feeling that God approved of his feelings for Caroline.

Caroline sat quietly, hands rested on her knees, as she let the wind hold her head up against the headrest, her mind wandering from flower-filled fields to ocean-front barbeques, all with her and Ryan together standing side by side as the perfect couple.

"Here it is. You ready to get a typewriter or what?" Ryan said with a quiet confidence stemming from the fact that he was able to find the pawn shop without getting lost, a feat that he usually could not claim success from.

"Yes, I think I see a blue one there in the window. How cool is that?" Caroline remarked as Ryan leaped out of the car and ran for her door, opening it with an air of enthusiasm usually reserved for prom dates and wedding night banquets.

"We've got two typewriters for every one computer. This is an antique shop, what did you expect?" the clerk said with a smile as he pointed to a shelf in the back of the store holding more than 30 typewriters.

"It's typewriter heaven, look at that," Ryan said to Caroline as they walked toward the large shelf.

I'm in heaven, Caroline thought as the feelings for this man she barely knew rushed through her veins. She was shopping, which didn't hurt her euphoria, either. Life was a prism of good and better, and she was the rainbow shining through it.

Black and brown typewriters lined the shelf from wall to wall. Old typewriters with vintage keys from the early 1900s sat next to automatic beige typewriters from the '80s.

"All those back there are in good working condition. I've tested each one of them myself," the man said from the counter.

"What about the blue one in the window, does that one work?" Caroline asked while turning to the man to see his response.

"Oh yes, that one works great, it's a beauty," the man said with a soft smile.

"What's your name?" Ryan asked while turning around himself to see the man.

"My name is Lenard, but you can call me Len," the man said gracefully as he rested his arms against the old wood checkout counter in the front of the store.

"You two antique collectors, or just looking to decorate your house with something unique?" Lenard blurted out, returning the personal question back to Ryan.

"Oh, we're not married. She just needs one for school," Ryan said, pointing to Caroline who was now in the window sitting on an old leather chest tapping the keys of the blue typewriter.

"Yes, it works. How much is it?" Caroline asked fearfully, knowing she had little money to her name that wasn't going to tuition already.

"For you, the price is one hug, and a promise to take good care of it," Lenard said, his eyes looking up at Caroline with admiration.

Caroline gently picked up the typewriter, handed it to Ryan, and walked to the front of the store. She stood face to face inches away from Lenard for several seconds, then she smiled and held him tightly.

"Thanks, I have no idea why or how you can give this to me, but it really means a lot, you have no idea," Caroline said as tears started to swell beneath her eyes.

"I have a feeling about you two, and I think this typewriter is meant to be with you both. Take good care of it for me," Lenard said, pushing away from Caroline to make his way back to his stool behind the counter.

"Are you sure you don't want anything, I'd be happy to pay you for it," Ryan said awkwardly as he walked to the counter.

"Nope, I've already got my payment. A beautiful girl like this, you'll need your money for other things my friend," Lenard said with a smile nodding at them both as the three stood in a triangle.

Caroline smiled, thanked Lenard again, and walked out the door. Ryan followed her out the door and into the car.

"Let's go out of town this weekend. I have always wanted to just go out of town at the spur of the moment, you know?" Ryan asked nervously as Caroline held the typewriter in her lap.

Caroline looked at Ryan, contemplating his request. Still euphoric from her typewriter gift, she nodded and smiled.

"OK, just don't tell me where we are going, I want it to be a surprise," Caroline said with a smile, as Ryan started the car.

Chapter 29: Designer Digital Footprint

Becker let out a slight groan of pleasure as he received a healthy scratching of his underbelly from a familiar pair of hands. Becker rubbed his white fur all over Caroline's black sweatpants as he lay in her lap, enjoying the precious moments of attention that drove him so wild.

Caroline cradled Becker with her arms as she sat at her makeshift table desk admiring her new typewriter.

"OK, Mr. Becker, it's time for mommy to do some work. Then we can watch The Bachelor tonight; I know how much you like that show," Caroline whispered to the small dog as she placed him on the floor.

Becker immediately assumed guard dog duties and sat at attention with his back touching Caroline's chair as he sat facing the door.

A single sheet of paper rested against the windowsill with two paragraphs of instructions on it. The instructions were from a sociology class requesting students to write about how different generations of people live differently.

Caroline's focus narrowed in on the keys of the typewriter as she pushed a single piece of paper into the machine and rolled the paper just enough to align perfectly with the keystrokes.

Caroline's fingers pressed, jotted, and tapped at the keys of her typewriter with the precession of a classical pianist. Her natural ability to write the words so deeply engrained in her day-to-day life was astounding.

Paragraph after paragraph, the typewriter continued to perform as Caroline let it all out. Becker sat quietly, facing the door as the duty was done. Every few minutes when a loud key was tapped, Becker's ears would perk up as he remained silent on the floor.

Something about sociology fascinated Caroline as she simultaneously wrote her assignment and realized a new and interesting perspective on her life.

"Oh my goodness, we've all lost our minds," Sandra said from the foot of Caroline's doorway, leaning her body through the narrow entrance while holding onto each side of the door with her hands for effect.

"Wow, you scared me!" Caroline said as she turned around, smiling from ear to ear.

"No, you are scaring me, what is that blue thing on your desk?" Sandra asked while walking toward her for a closer look.

Becker leaped up from his seated position and ran toward Sandra for some much-needed attention.

"It's a typewriter. You've never seen one before?" Caroline asked, allowing her smile to penetrate her usually serious demeanor.

"No, I've never seen one. I think my great grandfather used one before they invented the calculator," Sandra said with a chuckle.

Caroline sat still, not sure whether to cover her writing up or let her roommate see it.

"Well, I know you aren't serious about this typewriter thing. What, did you lose a bet or something?" Sandra said while pulling out a wooden stool from the corner of the room and placing it within inches of Caroline's chair.

"I'm no longer using computers, the Internet or any device that connects to the Internet." Caroline said with a tone mirrored only by police and school administrators.

"Wait, you aren't using a computer anymore?" Sandra asked with a puzzled look on her face.

"Nope, I think the Internet is a major violator of privacy and it can really distort your perception of people for no good reason," Caroline responded, the smile finally disappearing from her face.

"Sounds like somebody got caught on a porn site," Sandra noted as she looked around Sandra's room for signs of a secret addiction.

"No, Sandra, I wasn't caught on some porn site. I was screwed by my digital footprint. It's a long story," Caroline explained as she reached down to pet Becker for comfort.

"Wait, you have a digital footprint? So you can buy like digital shoes? Since they're not real, they must be cheaper—you could probably get a pair of Christian Louboutin shoes for nothing," Sandra rattled off without hesitation.

Caroline laughed as she slapped Sandra on the leg and moved closer to her ear.

"I met a boy the other day, and he's cute!" Caroline said to Sandra in a soft tone that only go louder with the final word of the sentence.

"Oh my goodness, Caroline. I knew you were glowing—you met a guy!" Sandra said immediately, forgetting about the serious talk that just occurred and putting a full-force focus on the new gossip she had just learned.

"Tell me more—how old, where is he from, what does he do, and when do I get to meet him?" Sandra asked.

Caroline sat quietly looking at Sandra's excitement=filled face. Her heart released pulses of happiness throughout her body, allowing her to feel as if she was cared about, as if someone really cared about her as a person.

"He's great. He's old but not too old, he's rich, and he's tall," Caroline responded in the same get louder as you go tone that puts the most accent on the last word.

"He's tall. Thank God, you met an angel!" Sandra shouted as she stood up from her stool.

"He's got a great job. He's definitely really nice, and he seems to have his act together," Caroline reasoned with Sandra as she stood with her hands on her hips.

"And he's tall!" Sandra said with a thundering clap of the hands.

"And he is tall," Caroline said in agreement as she rose to give Sandra a hug.

"Hey, and I'm going away with him this weekend. It's a surprise where we are going," Caroline whispered into Sandra's ear as they embraced.

Sandra quickly pushed Caroline enough to gain space between their two bodies.

"Can I come? No, I'm kidding," Sandra said with a smile, as she looked Caroline over for any indication of a practical joke being played on her.

"I'll get you a postcard. Now get out of here so I can finish this assignment for sociology class," Caroline said as she turned to her desk and fell into her chair.

Chapter 30: Wool Pants and Beef Jerky

"You can bring a dog on a plane?" Ryan asked with his head tilted to the side, eyeing the black leather dog carrier resting on the floor of Caroline's living room.

"Yes, you can carry it on like any other bag under a certain height and weight," Caroline said with a grin.

"OK, fair enough. Let's pack the pet on in there and get going," Ryan said, watching Becker circle in front of the door chasing his tiny tail.

"Sure, let me just grab my bag from upstairs," Caroline said as she leapt up the stairs toward her room.

Minutes passed as Caroline grabbed random item after random item in her room, stuffing them into her bag. She had only been on a few trips, and never one with a significant other, so it became top priority to pack everything she had ever imagined she would need into one oversized black duffle bag.

Caroline reached into her closet and in one swoop grabbed a down jacket, a pink bikini swimsuit, and a pair of wool pants, tossing them into her bag without a second thought.

A day-old, half-eaten bag of trail mix was sealed and thrown into a side pocket with a bag of beef jerky that had been sitting in her room for weeks. Taking a minute to catch her breath,

Caroline stood above the bag looking at its hodgepodge of items, laughing to herself, and zipped it up with one quick tug on the large, black metal zipper.

Muscling the bag back down the stairs, Caroline rested it at the foot while Ryan stood patiently in front of the door.

"OK, I think we are ready. I hope I packed enough shoes," Caroline said with a look of caution across her face.

"It's just a few days. I'm sure you've got enough shoes in that bag to last that long," Ryan said with a smile as he wrestled the large duffle back to his shoulder and out the door.

Caroline picked up Becker, slid him into his carrying case, and headed for the door.

Chapter 31: California

"California? California! California!" Caroline shouted loudly as Ryan handed her a plane ticket that showed a nonstop, first-class flight from Columbus, Ohio, to Los Angeles, California, on the front of it.

Ryan smiled as he picked up Caroline's large duffle bag and his own black travel bag, pushing the handle out from under it and letting the wheels of his bag assist him in getting to the departure terminal.

"Isn't California far away from here? I mean, wouldn't it be time to go home by the time we got there?" Caroline asked as she kept pace with Ryan walking across the jam-packed long-term airport parking garage.

Ryan swung his head back to look at Caroline in the eyes while he kept slowly walking forward, large luggage in tow.

"Well, it's about a five-hour flight, but it's a three-hour time difference, so basically I've got us going there early and leaving late, so we'll have a few full days out there to enjoy," Ryan said as he turned back around to face the approaching escalator that led to the departure terminal.

"Cool, so what are we doing there?" Caroline asked with a smile that inferred she no longer wanted to be surprised.

"It's a secret. All I can tell you is that I have it all planned out, and you'll love it," Ryan explained softly as he stood on the escalator.

Chapter 32: Aircraft Carrier

Seat 1A and 1B were side by side in the first row of the large aircraft. Each seat showed small creases of wear on the sides of the seats where leather tends to crack, but for the most part the seats were impeccable. The large, overstuffed headrest came with a built-in pillow. Sleek, black-rimmed, seven-inch LCD televisions rose out of the armrests for entertainment, and heated blankets slithered out of the armrest that bridged the two seats for those that got cold on the flight.

Caroline held Becker's carrier in her lap tightly as she closed her eyes and feel in love with seat 1B. The window to her right dripped enough sunlight into the plane that it tempted Caroline to look outside, but she remained seated face forward, head back with her eyes closed.

The excitement of her excursion with someone that seemed so sweet and so kind made her knees weak. She started to breathe heavily as she thought about going to a new place, a place she had never been, a place with such unimaginable possibilities like California.

Caroline's heart raced as she thought about holding Ryan's hand. She wanted to touch him so badly, but the awkwardness of it all was too much of a burden to bear. She had just met this person, she was normally so reserved, but felt so adventurous with him. Time stood still, her head bolted up, the wheels of the large aircraft had just touched the runway of LAX.

Chapter 33: Seat Back

"So, you have to tell me where we are going. I mean, we're headed there now, so it's not like I won't see," Caroline said with a playful smile as she sat in the passenger seat of a large sedan.

Ryan pushed his back into the driver's seat and played with the levers at the bottom left side of the chair, trying to adjust it for both comfort and safety.

"Do you know where the thing is to push this seat back?" Ryan asked as his knees seemed to touch his nose with the steering wheel of the car sitting in between them.

"I think it's that button on the side of the door, the one that shows the seat going back," Caroline said, demonstrating her quick wit.

Ryan laughed as he adjusted his seat while accelerating the car down a four-lane highway.

The nervousness was starting to overcome Ryan's usually cool and calm personality. He would think of something to say, but not be able to get it out for fear of Caroline thinking he was strange. He was so attracted to her both inside and out that he didn't want to jeopardize his chances by saying something stupid.

"We're going to this mountain outside of Santa Barbara, it's called Founder's Peak, and we're going camping!" Ryan blurted out while bracing for Caroline's reaction.

"Camping? That sounds scary. I hope Becker doesn't get eaten by any big bears," Caroline said with genuine concern as Becker sat quietly on her lap, glad to be out of his leather cage.

"No, this mountain is safe. It's a big tourist attraction. Travel magazines rated it one of the most beautiful mountain vacation destinations in the world. I'm sure Becker will be just fine," Ryan responded as his mind started to second guess the decision to book this trip instead of the one at the luxury spa in Las Vegas.

"OK, it sounds like an adventure," Caroline said while petting Becker's head.

Chapter 34: Space Blankets

Questions remained unanswered in Caroline's pragmatic mind. Where would the two of them sleep? She sure didn't see any sleeping bags in Ryan's small, designer luggage. Where they would eat? What would they do each day? All of these questions floated around Caroline's mind like a dozen balloons inflated with helium in a square box measuring four feet on all sides.

Caroline glanced at Ryan's hands on the steering wheel, his grip firm and poised. The confidence of his driving told her they'd be OK; no matter what happened, Ryan seemed to have a plan.

"Apparently the views from the mountain are incredible. You can see the city and the ocean from lots of points on it. The magazine recommended climbing to the top of the mountain to see this glass church built by a famous architect; it's apparently breathtaking," Ryan rattled off as he kept his eyes fixed on the road.

"That's interesting, sounds very majestic," Caroline said in an effort to show Ryan she was listening.

Caroline's mind drifted from place to place, still wondering what she would face on this mountain adventure. The anxiety was beyond her mental control; she felt nervous and nothing was going to change that feeling until she got to a safe place.

The four-lane highway dwindled into two and then into one as an hour and a half passed. Eventually, the green peak of the mountain started to penetrate the horizon that lay in the distant center of the car.

A small, brown sign indicated that Founder's Peak was open for campers as Ryan pulled the nondescript sedan into a parking space near the dirt trail at the foot of the mountain.

"We are here," Ryan said softly as Caroline opened her door and let Becker find a much-needed bush to relieve himself on.

"Great, so do we have sleeping bags?" Caroline asked nervously as if she'd been holding the question as long as Becker had been holding his urge to go to the bathroom.

"Well, sort of, Ryan said while climbing out of the car and moving toward the trunk of the sedan.

Ryan pulled out his backpack, and pulled out two yellow cylinders from the top of the bag. The cylinders resembled the tubes real estate agents store their flyers in when a home is for sale. He popped the top off one, and pulled out a thin yellow sheet.

"I got this from City Slickers, a camping store just down the street from my office building. These are space blankets, and they do all the warming of a large down blanket but take up 90% less space," Ryan proudly announced as Caroline eyed the paper-thin blanket.

"Space blankets? Why didn't you just pack a newspaper, that'd be about as warming as this thing," Caroline said with a hint of sarcasm as she ran her thin fingers across the edge of the blanket Ryan was holding up with two hands.

Ryan sat quietly on the lip of the bumper as he unfolded his next technological feat, a backpack skeleton that resembled a mini shower curtain rod. Ryan twisted each end of the small rod out and connected them together at the top and bottom to create a wearable backpack rack that would hold a single bag.

"This is what we put our bags on, isn't that cool?" Ryan said with a smile, holding the backpack skeleton in front of him for effect.

"My big duffle bag will fit on that?" Caroline asked as her eyes started to widen.

"Yes, it'll slide right on." Ryan said as he moved toward her bag to demonstrate.

Caroline and Ryan stood by the car as the sun started to disappear. The two took their time assembling their backpacks, and changing into more camping appropriate attire in the camping ground restroom on the other side of the parking lot.

"So, we aren't going to hike anywhere tonight are we?" Caroline asked as she tied her tennis shoes in a double knot and rolled the sleeves of an old flannel shirt up her arms tucking a pack of beef jerky in the left cargo pocket of her khaki pants.

"No, we're just going to go up the path a quarter mile or so to the campground, and that's it," Ryan explained, extending his arm and index finger toward the dark trail ahead of them.

Becker sat quietly near Caroline as his red leash was held tightly by Caroline's sweaty palm.

"OK, let's go," Caroline said as Becker led the two of them toward the dark trail.

Chapter 35: Happy Trails

Twilight quickly disappeared into pitch black night as four feet and four paws worked their way up the dirt path. Trees crowded the perimeter around the space they walked into a single-file trail that offered little difference in terrain than what lay on either side of it. Dead leaves crackled their last breaths of life as pair and their canine companion ascended up the path.

Acting on the assumption that the path would lead them to the picturesque camping ground Ryan had seen on the park Web site several days earlier, he forged forward long after the pedometer on his watch read a quarter mile in distance.

"It's been an hour, I can't see anything, and my feet are killing me," Caroline let out with a sigh of frustration exacerbated to Yale School of Drama caliber.

"Well the guide said only a quarter mile, but I wasn't sure if we were walking slowly with these somewhat heavy bags on our back so that it was just taking us longer to walk that length," Ryan explained while turning to Caroline to expose his sweat-drenched face and T-shirt.

"There were two spots back there where the trail seemed to fork. I couldn't tell if it was just a little resting place or an actual new trail, but maybe the camping grounds are back there?" Ryan asked with an air of defeat penetrating his usually calm voice.

Caroline stood motionless while she released the overstuffed duffle bag that had been strapped to her back onto the trail. Her heart started to race; she felt vulnerable in her newfound circumstances.

"Are you doing OK?" Ryan asked softly, placing his hand on Caroline's forearm.

"I am in the middle of nowhere with a person I don't really know, in a state I've never been to, on a mountain that apparently gets very dark and scary after the sun goes down, while looking for a campground I have never seen. How do you think I am doing?" Caroline rebutted with a roar as she plopped down on her duffle bag in a frustrated protest.

Ryan squatted down on his knees as if he'd been the starting catcher for the New York Yankees in a past life and started to whisper.

"I know it's frustrating, I know this is scary, I'm a little freaked out, too. But we will be fine, we'll just wait till the sun comes up and retrace our steps. We haven't gone that far—worst case, we'll wind up back at the car and grab a hotel in Santa Barbara," Ryan pleaded as he gazed into Caroline's soft eyes.

The two starred at each other quietly for several minutes, Ryan gently caressing Caroline's hair as she started to stretch out on top of her duffle bag.

"You want the space blanket?" Ryan asked with a smile.

"What do you think?" Caroline mouthed as her eyes shut closed in unison with a deep exhale.

Chapter 36: Armpit Bigfoot

Becker tucked his nose beneath Caroline's armpit to shield his eyes from any unruly sights. Never much of an outdoor dog, Becker's heart was on fire with thoughts of snakes and out of control apes coming down the narrow path he lay on for a doggy dinner delight.

Ignoring all the plausible scenarios, Becker choose to focus on the most farfetched ones. Sea creatures out of water, reptiles with massive lizard tongues, even Bigfoot crept into the dog's tiny head.

Ryan tossed his sweat-soaked T-shirt off to the side of the trail as he climbed into a cocoon-shaped yellow blanket. The tip of the shirt hit Becker in the back.

Becker turned his head slightly just enough to see what had touched him. His body remained still as his eyes darted from one side of the socket to the other. A small group of white teeth emerged from his black lips; Becker wanted to let any intruder that might be lurking behind him know that this dog had bite. He burrowed deeper into the armpit of Caroline as she started to hiss a gentle chorus of sleep sounds.

Hours passed with no movement from any of them, all asleep and far more relieved in their current state than when they had been awake. Drifting into dreams of life and love, they slept quietly, until they were suddenly awakened by a thunderous noise at 5:32 in the morning.

Chapter 37: Righteous Rain

A hissing wind picked up Ryan's black and red nylon backpack and deposited it on the other side of the mountain out of his sight. Ryan sprung to his feet as the wind started to push the leaves off of the trees in a circular motion that resembled a desert storm.

Drips of water started to fall in pearl shapes from all corners of the sky as Caroline jolted to her feet.

"I can't sleep with this noise!" Caroline shouted as her eyes opened to see Ryan and Becker both standing at full attention in front of her.

"I mean what is going on?" Caroline worriedly corrected herself as Ryan started to jog past her into the deep woods.

"Where are you going? What are you doing?" Caroline yelled as the wind and rain started to pelt them with a steady spray of cold air and wet droplets that only a mountain in California can produce so quickly.

"I'm going to get my backpack, the wind took it over this way. Just stay put and hold all our stuff together," Ryan said pointing into a sea of trees as he increased his jog to a sprint and turned away from Caroline.

Becker started to moan an anxious series of noises as the rain turned his usually soft, white coat into a thin strain of wet hair on his tiny body that exposed his pale, pink skin.

"It's OK, Becks. I've got to get all our stuff together, so you just sit here and be a good dog," Caroline said as she started to digest the gravity of the situation.

A series of stadium-sized clouds started to form over the horizon. Second by second, the clouds marched toward the area where Caroline was busy collecting all that belonged to her and Ryan, assembling it in a neat pile under a redwood tree that was shielding Becker from the increasingly rapid pace of raindrops falling from the sky.

Without warning, the temperature dropped from a mild 62 degrees to a bristling 38 in what seemed like less than a minute. Birds that had been humming their morning music suddenly were nonexistent. Caroline returned to the redwood tree, and softly sat underneath it in shock.

"Come here, Becker. Let's keep each other warm, kiddo," Caroline said as she reached out and grabbed the dog in an effort to remain calm.

Becker slipped into her arms, raising his eyes to meet hers as if to let her know whatever storm was coming he'd be there to go through it with her. It was as if he was telling her that if he could be rescued and put into a warm safe place, he wouldn't, not without his owner, not without mom.

Thunder announced its arrival with two vibrating thrusts of bass-filled snap sounds that forced Becker to dig his head deep into Caroline's now-folded arms.

"Where are you, Ryan?" Caroline yelled as the rain started to pour, soaking Caroline's thin clothing to a state of see-through and masking the steady flow of tears dripping down her face.

A deafening roar followed a flash of light that forced Caroline to look up to the sky. Three seconds passed;, the mountain went silent.

Caroline closed her eyes, and started to wonder what she had done to deserve this. She thought of all the times she missed church as a child for frivolous reasons. She thought of all the people she had spoken badly about in her life. She thought about the few people that she could honestly call an enemy. She opened her eyes and tilted her head up to the sky to see a reddish-brown blur approaching at an incredible speed. It was falling directly toward her at a rate that suggested she had no time to move. Caroline's head snapped back, her body went limp, and the storm carried on.

Chapter 38: Backwards Beast

Two peas and a pod of luggage, Ryan kept thinking as he back-peddled deeper into the woods while keeping his eye on the makeshift campground they had formed on the trail that lay far in the distance. He knew that he had got them lost once already, and he wasn't prepared to get lost again. The rain that dripped off his shoulder blades that would normally hit the ground was being carried by the wind in all directions. His usually kept hair pointed in every direction as he pushed it away from his forehead to keep his eyes fixed on the campground in the distance.

Back-peddling slowly, Ryan got into a rhythm of taking one step back, looking right, looking left, looking back at the trail, and then taking another step. After all, the backpack couldn't be that far away from where they had been sleeping. How far could a single gust of wind carry the thing. he thought.

Minutes passed, and his steps remained measured and slow against the feverish winds and cold rain.

Blood pulsated through Ryan's veins as the proactive, aggressive, "take no prisoners" attitude started to return. Ryan was mild mannered at work and with friends, but most people knew he had a side to him, that if certain buttons were pushed, the beast would come out. The person that had grown up neglected, angry, and worst of all, privileged would come out. It was the side of a person that, when left to his own survival, would do anything to stay alive. It was the gut instinct of a man that has a will to live, where surviving a situation becomes paramount to anything else in life. With each bolt of lightning, his swagger grew more intense. He would not die on this mountain, and he would not lose the girl of his dreams either.

Ryan turned around reluctantly as the wind picked up; he reasoned it was impossible to keep back-peddling in the storm without falling over. The wind was pushing his body forward as he back-peddled, increasing the chance he'd fall over if he kept going against the grain. With one turn and two more steps, the makeshift campground went out of sight.

Chapter 39: Motion Sick

Becker's nose sniffed the wine barrel size branch that lay atop of Caroline's narrow body. His tail wagged feverishly as the storm started to wane. Rain drops stopped falling as the sun reappeared from a series of dissolving clouds above.

Caroline's body lay motionless under the large branch as Becker started to wander away from the trail. Sensing fear, the dog went in search of something, anything that might bring life back to his closest friend.

Each step Becker took away from the trail increased the level of the dog's anxiety. Once the trail was out of his immediate line of sight, he started to run in any direction. He ran until his tiny lungs couldn't take anymore. There was nothing but trees and bushes, and no humans, nothing. Becker kept moving like a dog that would not be deterred.

A fresh trail appeared, and a scent of the familiar passed his nose ever so slightly. He stopped, turned, and noticed a human he had never seen before. It was time to alert.

Becker started to bark, barking like he had never barked before, letting all the eons of emotion that crowded his veins and burdened his heart out in a series of loud barks.

The human took notice. Two black boots started to approach Becker. Now all the dog had to do was guide him back to his friend.

Chapter 40: Kickball

Caroline felt a familiar cushion on top of her bare feet. As her eyes slowly opened with her head hanging down, she noticed Becker sitting atop of her bare feet. His tail was wagging and his eyes met hers. She felt a relief; she was in a haze and seeing her dog was one thing that helped her come back to reality.

As her blurry vision started to cease, Caroline looked around and noticed all the bags were gone from under the tree that was now in the distance. She felt a throbbing pain on the top left part of her head as she tried to move her hands to scratch her back that felt like it was on fire, but she couldn't. As hard as she tried, her hands were stuck.

Caroline sat propped up atop a fallen tree with her back resting against an upright tree. As she looked herself over, a cold rush of fear shot through her veins. She was naked. How did the storm do this, she wondered as she finally cleared her vision enough to look at her hands, which were bound by rope together tied in a grip that people make when they pray.

Feeling a combination of fear and humiliation, Caroline struggled to try to cover herself with her legs and elbows by pushing her body forward and legs up.

"Hello there lady. What's your name?" asked a bearded man standing behind Caroline with a whisper into her ear as he looked her over, obviously noticing her sudden movement.

"Aren't you just the prettiest thing in the whole wide world? Looks like you had a little accident," the man said to Caroline with a Southern twang that suggested he wasn't a native of California.

Caroline sat still, not saying a word and trying not to gag from the putrid body order that was wafting from the burly man now standing directly in front of her. She looked down at her feet and noticed they were not tied. A feeling of hope briefly fell over her as she realized that there might be a chance for survival.

"Looks to me like you bumped your head over there," the man said as he pointed his thin, wrinkled finger toward a trail less than 30 feet away.

"Who are you, and what the hell are you doing?" Caroline said in a frightened whisper that barely made its way to the man's ear who was now standing within inches of her face.

"You can call me your husband, because we are about to make a baby," the man said as he placed his wrinkled, dirt-stained hand on Caroline's bare, white shoulder.

Shivers shot through her body as he started to unbutton his pants. Caroline braced herself for whatever was to come next. She took a deep breath, tensed her muscles, and exploded with a right kick that hit the man squarely in his groin.

"Ouch, I can't believe, oh you little, dirty…" the main mumbled as he fell to the ground in a fetal position.

Caroline felt the urge to run, but didn't know if it was the right time to do so. She only had one chance to get it right, and the calculated side of her said to wait until she could do further damage to this person, damage that would give her enough time to really make a run for it without him catching up and killing her.

Chapter 41: Paradise Island

In a leap of faith, Ryan sat down and looked up to the sky. To his surprise, a red and black backpack hung from a branch directly above him.

"How about that? No wonder I couldn't find it on the ground," Ryan rationalized out loud as he looked the tree over.

A series of large rocks lay beneath the tree. An image of a baseball player pitching a fastball ran through his mind as he picked one up.

With brute force, Ryan tossed the rock at the tree and knocked the backpack off the branch. It fell into his hands, along with a sense of success Ryan hadn't felt in days.

He turned around and started to retrace his steps, literally. Each footprint he had left he put his feet back into, walking slowly to make sure he did not go off course.

Ryan's footprints easily stood out in the fresh mud of the storm-soaked mountain; even the Nike swoosh logo on the bottom of his sneakers was visible in most of his shadowy footprints in the mud. Ryan continued on for 25 minutes, taking step after step thinking of how frightened Caroline must be not knowing where he went.

An image crept into Ryan's head of a cruise boat just off the coast of Nassau Island in the Bahamas. He had been once as a college student, and always thought it would be nice to return with the girl of his dreams to share the ocean views, the quaint tourist traps, and the pulsating night life with someone other than a bunch of his guy friends. With someone special, with someone he could marry. He thought about Caroline's soft skin soaking in the Caribbean sun, her flawless, toned body donning a skimpy bikini. He was totally at peace.

Chapter 42: Do Something

After nearly an hour, Ryan had the feeling he was almost back to the trail where he had last seen Caroline. The footprints were leading him in the right direction, and soon he'd see her again, apologize for everything that went wrong, and they'd find a way off of this mountain. His thoughts of a pleasurable reuniting quickly ceased when he noticed a footprint of a large boot freshly put in the mud.

"It's too big to be Caroline's footprint," Ryan proclaimed out loud as if to cue the person that had just created this print for an introduction.

The mountain remained silent; Ryan analyzed the print for a minute, and figured it was a park ranger that had come to help them. He followed the new set of footprints. Wherever they led, Ryan was confident that was where Caroline would be as well.

Each step Ryan took had him hearing new things. First it was the sound of leaves crackling, similar to what he heard the day before when they were walking together on the path. Then it was the sound of a man, in the distance, yelling something. Finally the sounds were met by sight. A wave of adrenaline crested inside Ryan. He saw a women's bare back pushed up against a tree; he knew something was terribly wrong.

Ryan took a minute to gather the facts. The clever and often cynical journalist in him took over. Assume the worst, prepare for the worst, know that people are capable of doing very bad things, Ryan kept telling himself over and over in his head.

He removed his shoes and placed them to the side. He wanted to approach with as little sound as possible. He took inventory of the situation as he approached.

It took just five more steps for Ryan to see Caroline's dark, long hair resting on the middle of her back. He could see a figure, a man, wearing a blue and white flannel shirt and an old pair of jeans that looked like they were undone getting up off the floor.

His heart beat like it was going to come out of his chest if he didn't take action soon. He knew exactly what was going on, and he had to do something now, before it was too late.

The thought of Caroline getting raped made his eyes widen with anger. His palms started to sweat, he was not going to let another girl get raped on his watch. An incident in college when a person he knew raped his own girlfriend at the time in his bed had never left him. The trauma she went through, the doubters in court, the life she had once lived had forever been tarnished. He was not going to let it happen again, even if it meant he had to die to stop it from happening, it would not happen again.

Chapter 43: Harm's Way

A grapefruit-sized rock lay to the left of Ryan as he stood less than 100 feet from the man that was now undressing himself in front of a naked and shaking Caroline.

Ryan, scanning the perimeter for an entry point, knew there was only seconds left until the unthinkable would happen. Tossing a calculated and well thought-out entrance from behind the tree out the window because it was too far of a distance to approach, Ryan realized his only chance of saving Caroline was to charge in from where he was standing and try to knock the animal out with a rock. An image of a Native American tribesman fighting for his life came to Ryan's mind. Fresh face paint from the Native American's face mixed with sweat and blood dripping off onto a dead man below graced his mind. The warrior in him awoke, and it was now time to let it out.

"I'm over here!" Ryan yelled in an adrenaline-charged voice while running full speed toward the man.

All fear had left Ryan, a rare trait that he had always possessed. Ryan had the ability to eliminate fear and anxiety in the most strenuous situations. It was as if he had been made to thrive in the absolute horrid of times.

Rock in hand, Ryan knew he had one chance to hit this

person square in the face, but he first had to get Caroline out of harm's way.

"Run, you have to go now. Don't look back, just run!" Ryan screamed to Caroline as she stood up and ran away as fast as she could, Becker following her in stride.

Ryan took the rock and heaved it as fast as he could toward the man's head without breaking his pace.

The man ducked, and the rock missed him by several inches, but Ryan kept running at him.

"You want some of this, come and get it," Ryan taunted as he prayed for the man to come closer, knowing with each step the man took toward him, Caroline would be one more step toward safety.

Ryan pushed his fist toward the man's face, connecting squarely with his jaw. The man fell to the floor. Ryan knew he had to buy time, at least five to 10 minutes to give Caroline enough time to get to safety.

"You want to be involved in a rape? I'll make your dreams come true, pal," Ryan said, pushing the man's face into the dirt and stripping off his pants.

"I'm going to rape you, how do you like that?" Ryan yelled as the beast within came out. He punched the man in the back of the head 12 times, not stopping to breathe. The man lay still, and Ryan took a step back to assess the situation.

Blood poured out from Ryan's hand as the man rolled over, pulled out a handgun, and fired a bullet directly in Ryan's shoulder.

"I'm not going to let you rape me. I'm going to kill you, and then I'm going to go find your pretty friend, and well, you know what I will do to her," the man said, rising to his feet as if the punches to the back of his head were nothing more than a stoke to his evil fire of dementia.

Ryan lay flat on his back, gasping for air, watching the man appear above his body preparing to execute him.

"Kill me, but you will never touch her, I promise you that," Ryan said, looking the man directly in his eyes as if it were the last words that would come from his mouth.

Chapter 44: It's Not Over

Looking down the barrel of the gun pointing at his head, three words rang in Ryan's ear: it's not over. Ryan looked up at the man, but his mouth was shut. Who had said that to him? what did it mean, he wondered. Was it God? Ryan had casually believed in a higher being, but wasn't sure what to think growing up. He felt the words grace his ears again: it's not over. He felt a sudden bolt of energy throughout his body.

Ryan pushed himself up, punched the man in the stomach, and grabbed the gun from his hands, swinging it 20 feet away into a patch of leaves on the ground.

The man's head bobbed up after Ryan had hit him in the stomach. Ryan put all of his might into a right-handed punch that sent the man tumbling to the ground in pain.

"This is not going to get you out of here. I'll still kill you," the man said while pushing himself up off the ground as if he'd been in similar battles in the past and won.

Ryan knew at this very moment he could run away, possibly escape the man, but they both knew he wouldn't. He needed to know that he did everything in his power to save Caroline, and that meant fighting to the death, at least that is what Ryan kept thinking.

Drums pounded in Ryan's mind. Instead of just one warrior, there were now dozens dancing in victorious strides around a pit of fire. One warrior turned to Ryan and said, "It's not over."

The two men scrambled toward the gun, Ryan grabbing the intruder's boot and twisting it in an effort take him down. They both fell to the ground.

"It's not over, it's not over, it's not over," Ryan kept screaming as he held the man's leg to the floor so he couldn't reach the handgun laying inches from the tips of his fingers.

Dust rose from the ground as the warrior chants grew louder in Ryan's head. Was he delirious, he wondered, as the mental volume knob kept turning louder and louder. The warriors spoke to him again, telling him in unison now, "It's not over."

"It's about to be," the man said, pushing so close to the gun his fingernails grazed the black metal handle.

Chapter 45: I Will Not Let You Die

Caroline looked into her hands and found a T-shirt and mesh gym shorts balled up in them. Did Ryan give them to her? Did she grab them? How did she get these things in her hands was a question she could not answer as she quickly put them on to cover her naked body.

She had only run several hundred yards away from where she had been attacked, but she couldn't go any further—not out of fatigue, but out of a strong and relentless feeling that she had to go back and help Ryan.

She paced back and forth between two large trees, Becker following at her motions with his head as he sat in front of her.

"I've got to go back, Becks. I can't leave him there," Caroline said to the dog as if her life wasn't in danger.

"I can't go back, Becks. That man is going to rape me and kill me," Caroline said as she came to her senses.

Becker sat quietly as Caroline paced, her blood boiled over in a rage that caused her to want to fight instead of flee. The absolute horror that she had experienced was causing her to feel wronged, to feel abused, to feel angry. She wanted to help Ryan fight this beast; she had to help Ryan fight this man.

"We're going back," Caroline said as she spit a mouthful of

blood onto the ground in front of her.

Before the words had finished leaving her mouth, Caroline had started to run back into the fire.

Long stride after long stride, Caroline moved with gazelle-like speed through the mix of trees and brush as Becker galloped behind her.

Her mind raced. She was terrified and wanted to run for help, but a feeling trumped her terror that made her want to go back. Something primal compelled her to fight. She would not let Ryan die, not without a fight at least.

She kept hearing a voice telling her something, in a tone as soft as a whisper yet as firm as the loudest words she'd ever heard spoken. I will not let you die. Who said that, she questioned. Who won't let me die?

The voice calmed her. She knew it was God. She knew her time to save Ryan had come. A purpose fell over her so powerful and she no longer was afraid.

Chapter 46: Shinobi

Approaching the camp site, Caroline slowed down her sprint-like running pace and saw a pool of blood with Ryan laying in it face down on the ground. He was still moving, the man stood over him kicking him in the ribs as he commanded him to give up.

"You still love her now? You still want to be the hero now, boy?" the man shouted as he toyed with Ryan's life.

Ryan pushed his leg back enough to kick the man in the shin. Ryan forced himself to his feet, his body dripped a seemingly unending amount of blood as he pushed his weight into the man and they both tumbled over a rock.

Caroline looked to her left and noticed Ryan's backpack shell's steel frame glistening above the leaves. She bolted toward it, rolled off one steel rod, and crouched behind a large rock.

She opened Ryan's backpack and pulled out the stick of beef jerky she had given to him a day earlier still in its wrapping. She unwrapped it, looked at Becker, ran the stick of jerky underneath his nose, and threw it as hard as she could toward Ryan. The beef jerky flew above the two of them and landed five feet behind them at the foot of a large tree.

Becker understood his duty and ran mightily toward the stick, causing both Ryan and the intruder to look up and see what was going on. Becker ran past them in eager pursuit of the jerky.

Caroline appeared behind the man with the metal shaft in hand and took a baseball swing at his head, connecting with a force that she did not know she had in her. Caroline immediately pushed Ryan to the side, kicked the gun with her bare foot, and gripped the man's neck from behind; locking the bar and her two arms around his neck.

"Ahhhh!" Caroline screamed with a fire-filled emotion as she held onto the man's back, choking him with the backpack skeleton shaft.

The intruder quickly rose to his feet, but Caroline would not let go, hanging on to his back and tightening her grip.

"I will not let you kill him. I will not let you take him from me, you…" Caroline shouted as she drove her frail knee into his back.

The man started to feverishly turn in circles, causing Caroline to fall off his back. Before she hit the ground she recoiled her legs and leaped back onto him, this time wrapping her left forearm around his neck and using the metal rod in her right hand to beat his ribs. Wallop after wallop, she keep hitting him in the ribs; Ryan couldn't believe it.

While Caroline had the intruder in a perpetual chokehold, Ryan crawled toward the man's pants laying on the ground. He ripped a piece of the pant leg off with his teeth and started to wrap it around his shoulder. Ryan knew that if he didn't cut off the bleeding from his shoulder soon, he'd bleed to death.

Caroline wound up and smashed the man's knee with the steel rod, causing him to yelp in pain and crumble to the floor. Caroline climbed off of him, stood to her feet, took both hands on the rod, and delivered a punishing blow to his head.

A roaring thump distributed Ryan's shoulder wrapping as the shaft met the man's face, his skin instantly turning to a blood red color that left no doubt he had been seriously injured by the blow.

"I think I knocked him out," Caroline said to Ryan, brushing the dirt and blood off of her face.

"You're incredible, I had no idea you were so skilled with a sword," Ryan said with a smile as he pushed his body up against a tree stump tying off the cloth around his shoulder as tightly as he could.

"You've been shot!" Caroline said with wide eyes as she fell to her knees in front of Ryan.

"Yeah, he got me in the shoulder. I'm just trying to cut the bleeding off here," Ryan grunted as he handed Caroline a second piece of the denim pant leg he had been trying to wrap himself with.

Caroline immediately got to work wrapping his shoulder as tight as she could, taking a clip she had left in her hair from the day before and using it to keep the bandage tight.

"I can't believe you came back," Ryan said to Caroline as he closed his eyes and passed out on the ground.

Chapter 47: Alive

Holding the gun against his head Caroline couldn't help but think about pulling the trigger. She'd learned how to fire a pistol from her father years ago, and she knew exactly how to kill this man in an instant. She also was aware that he would most likely try to kill her and Ryan if she didn't do it to him first.

It had never occurred to her that her attacker wasn't lost in the woods like they were. It had never occurred to Caroline that the attacker might have something they could use to get to safety, not until she was starring him in the face with a gun to his head. All of a sudden she realized, this disgusting person held the key to her and Ryan getting out of the forest alive.

Ryan needed medical attention soon or he'd bleed to death. Caroline had seen enough medical dramas on TV to know that as a statement of truth. Caroline had to act fast, before the man woke up, before Ryan died. She needed to do something.

Caroline stood up, looked around the now disheveled camp site, and looked for clues—clues to get off the mountain and to safety, she thought as she sifted through an old nylon tent apparently belonging to her attacker. A dirty canvas bag sat flat at the back of the tent. Caroline grabbed it, pulled it out of the tent, and moved back in front of the man with the gun to his head in case he awoke from his forced slumber.

With her right hand holding the gun extended, she used her left to sort through the bag. A three-page pamphlet caught Caroline's eye. She thought it could possibly be a map.

The pamphlet headline read, A Glass Church in the Sky, and a full-color photo of a large, glass church atop a mountain graced the cover. The top of the mountain looked narrow and grassy, without much obstructing the church.

Caroline stood up, put the handgun in her back pocket, and walked over to Ryan. Leaning down, she placed her lips two inches from Ryan's right ear.

"There is nothing up there but the church, you can't miss it, so that's where we have to go," Caroline whispered to Ryan as he slowly awoke.

"Can you walk?" Caroline said to Ryan as he came to a hazy state of consciousness.

"I can give it a try," Ryan said softly as Caroline reached out her arm and helped him to his feet.

"I love you," Ryan mumbled to Caroline as she put his arm over her shoulder, and held on to his hand so he wouldn't let go.

Chapter 48: Shocking Revelation

Contrary to finding the camp grounds, there was a simple and direct way to the top of the mountain—go up. Caroline held Ryan's backpack in her left hand as she gripped Ryan's half-limp body in her right. Becker walked behind Caroline using his two front paws to push Ryan's feet forward when they would stop moving, which happened every few minutes.

"I need you to wake up, and try to walk on your own," Caroline said firmly to Ryan who stumbled forward falling to his knees.

"I can't carry you up this entire mountain. You have to help me here," Caroline yelled to Ryan in his dazed state as if she were talking to a ghost.

Ryan fell face down to the ground, as Caroline surveyed how far they'd gone from the site of the horrific incident. It couldn't have been more than 500 feet, Caroline thought to herself as she tried to muster up a way to get them both to safety.

Caroline had once read that small volts of electricity can cause people to return to states of consciousness for a short period of time. If Ryan was able to wake up, even for 30 minutes they could make enough progress to get to safety for the night. Caroline dropped to the ground, emptied out the backpack, and look for something that could electrocute her friend.

Chapter 49: Toss Up

Sifting through a half-dozen items that were packed in the bag, nothing looked even remotely close to doing the job. A comb, notepad and a box of pens lay in front of Caroline as she sat Indian style next to Ryan's limp body that had been turned over and covered with the small space blanket for warmth.

There has to be something here, Caroline kept thinking as she pet a passed out Becker in her lap. Minutes passed, but Caroline kept hope alive, sifting through the items in the backpack, the only one of which that seemed useful was a half-full bottle of spring water.

A pain knifed through Caroline's abdomen with incredible force. She rose to her feet and moved toward a bush, tripping on a hard object in a side pocket of the backpack, throwing up what little was left in her stomach on top of the bush.

Caroline lay on the ground, cringing in pain. Her stomach was empty, her body feeling dehydrated, and she feared she was coming down from the shock of the whole incident. She needed to act fast before she passed out.

Looking back at her feet, she noticed the side pocket that she had tripped over was now showing a black metal device. She rushed over and pulled the device from the bag.

"An electric shaver, thank God," Caroline shouted out loud as she pulled a battery-powered electric shaver from a side pocket in Ryan's backpack.

Wasting no time, Caroline peeled off the black protective top to the shaver and shoved a pen into the top of the shaver, forcing the blade to pop out the top and fall to the ground. Caroline sprinkled a drop of water on the top of the shaver, letting it fall into the middle of the device. A faint, blue light shimmered for a second. Could it have been an electric current, Caroline wondered as she prepared to try to shock Ryan back to life.

"Get back, Becker. I'm not sure what is going to happen when I do this," Caroline shouted to Becker as she pushed the half-asleep dog away from her and Ryan.

Chapter 50: Up and Onward

Not knowing whether she was about to revive or kill the man, Caroline took a minute to think about her plan to rescue Ryan.

The forest went silent. Caroline poured over the possible scenarios. She could kill Ryan with the makeshift shock treatment if she did what she was thinking about doing. She could try to get him up the mountain, but that wasn't going to happen as the sheer weight of a grown man on her shoulders was too much for her to handle. They could sit and wait for help, but that might be days before anyone came, and what if the bastard from the camp found them, then they'd surely be dead.

Scenario after scenario played out in Caroline's mind, none of them seemed promising. She was not a doctor, she had no experience with injuries, trauma, or how much blood loss is lethal. She just knew she had to do something.

A crackle broke her concentration as she felt a slight shock on her fingers. Looking down expecting to see two pieces of clothing causing static cling, she noticed the electric razor was in her hand, her wet finger was resting atop of it.

If that isn't a sign, I don't know what is, Caroline thought as flipped the razor on high, pulled Ryan's shirt up, and released the cap of the water bottle.

Caroline carefully poured a small bit of water on Ryan's stomach, and closed her eyes as she pressed the razor to his chest.

"Ahhhh," Ryan yelled as he leapt to his feet, knocking Caroline on her back.

"I wasn't trying to hurt you, I was trying to wake you up," Caroline yelled with her hands in the air so as to block any retaliation Ryan might offer up.

"I'm up, I am up. Where are we?" Ryan asked as he picked up his bag like he'd never been shot.

"We need to get to the top of the mountain, as fast as possible," Caroline said pointing toward a sea of trees that seemingly rose to the sky.

Caroline pushed herself off the ground, collected the contents of the backpack, and started to walk up the mountain. Ryan and Becker followed her as she kept a brisk pace.

Hours of hiking directly up the mountain in the now pitch black and cold California night had exhausted Caroline. She rested her arms on Ryan's shoulder as he pushed forward.

"I know you are tired, but we can't stop now, we have to keep going," Ryan said to Caroline as he wrapped her arms around his neck and held them tightly.

"I'm fine, I am just a little tired but I can make it," Caroline said as she held a panting Becker in her right arm.

Another two hours passed as their effort continued to the summit of the mountain. Each step began to slow as Caroline nodded off in Ryan's arms while still moving her legs forward, awaking only when Becker's hind legs would kick her stomach as her grip loosened on him.

"Let's stop here," Ryan said, knowing if he did not make the choice to rest now their bodies would do it for them soon enough.

    Caroline fell to the ground without muttering a word. Ryan put his arms around her, took out the paper thin blanket, and wrapped it around the two of them. Becker positioned himself at the feet of the two bodies facing the trail they had just come up as if to watch for trouble. Within seconds, they were all asleep.

Chapter 51: I Love You

Within an hour of falling asleep, Ryan awoke to a throbbing pain in his shoulder. He could feel the top part of his shoulder going numb, and feeling in his left arm started to wane as well. His eyes winded as he took in the cool California air and considered his fate.

Caroline lay motionless next to Ryan, breathing a steady cadence of breathes that was indicative of a deep sleep. Ryan gazed at her, a piece of excitement returning to his otherwise horrified mind state.

Ryan's eyes gazed into the sky, sorted through the tree tops above him, and the microscopic rays of light that were constructed of light from the stars mixing with the tears in his eyes.

Starved, beaten, bloody, uprooted, lost, and alone, Caroline's beauty was as great as it'd ever been. Her hair glimmered in the night sky, reflections of the moon danced on her loose hair that was gently blowing in the wind. Her lips remained parsed just enough to let the gasps of breathe in and out of her exceptional body. Ryan sat in awe, knowing if he was to die on this mountain, he'd have just left the world when it was at its best for him. Every bit of Caroline's body was something he wanted to be with for the rest of his life, and something inside him told him he would.

"It's time to go, kiddo," Ryan said to Caroline while caressing her cheek softly with his dirt-encrusted, blood-stained right hand.

Chapter 52: Push

As much as he tried, Ryan could not get Caroline to wake up. She would mumble words of no meaning, and push her hands forward, as if she were fighting with fatigue to let her come back to reality, but it was a losing battle. After several failed tries at getting Caroline up, Ryan knew it was up to him to take her to the mountain top.

Opening Caroline's mouth, Ryan poured what little water he had left in his bottle into her mouth. He packed the blanket into his backpack, lifted Becker into his right hand, and pushed his shoulder underneath Caroline's body, balancing her form over his shoulder. Ryan stood up, Caroline's weight forcing him to regain his balance several times before moving forward. With Caroline on his back and Becker clutched in his right hand, he continued his ascent to the top of the mountain.

Grunting after each step, Ryan moved up the mountain slowly, shifting the weight of Caroline's body from shoulder to shoulder every minute or two in an attempt to relieve his overwhelming fatigue.

The eight-pound Becker started to feel like a 100-pound dumbbell in Ryan's right hand as he worked his way up a nondescript trail on the mountain. Ryan took a canvas strap of the backpack that remained fixed to his back and tied a knot with it on the right side of his belt. He rested Becker's body on the strap, and tightened it to secure the dog to the side of his body.

With his right hand now free, Ryan used both to keep his balance as the incline on the mountain steepened. The mountain at this point was so steep, Ryan was able to touch the face by simply reaching out his arms and leaning over several inches. His trek was now a vertical climb, and he had no choice but to keep moving.

Sweat poured off of Ryan's body as he forcefully moved ahead with each step. After several consecutive steps, Ryan would pause for air, and then go back into climbing, careful not to fall backwards in the process.

Push, Ryan kept thinking, he had to push. Thoughts of his high school years came into his mind as it eagerly left the dire straits reality of his current circumstances.

Ryan pictured himself in the old high school gym he spent so much time in as a kid, standing inside a squat rack with the large, Olympic size bar on his back full of 45-pound plates and his best friend, Ronnie Stevens, in his ear yelling the word push to him over and over again.

The image kept with Ryan as he willed his body to take each step forward using his outstretched arms for balance on the steep mountain.

Sweating in nothing but a tank top and gym shorts, Ryan would take the weight of three men on his shoulders and drop into a full squat, pressing his way back to standing posture. Those days Ryan had something to prove. Images of onlookers marveling at Ryan's thin frame negotiating such large amounts of weight up and down in his high school gym gave Ryan hope.

The grit had not left Ryan. This visualization invigorated Ryan, and he kept thinking of Ronnie Stevens yelling the word push, willing him not to give up.

Chapter 53: There Will Be Light

A single bird let out a slight chirp that startled Ryan. He looked around. Could anyone be there? What was that noise, he wondered as he kept moving forward.

Five minutes passed. Ryan grunted his way five more steps up the mountain and two birds chirped. Ryan didn't know what to think.

"Help, help me," Ryan said in a soft, raspy voice while resting his two hands on the mountain.

"Is anyone there?" Ryan asked with what could have been his last breathe while his body started to give out from underneath him.

"I am here, I was here, and I am here, and I will always be here, " a voice said from a distance.

"Who are you?" Ryan asked, pretty sure he already knew the answer.

"You know who I am. The question is, do you accept me now?" the voice said with an increasing clarity that startled Ryan to his knees while Caroline's body still rested on his back.

"Yes Lord, I accept you. I need you God. I can't live without you," Ryan said with a passion he did not know was still left in him.

"You are almost there, my son. Keep going. I will deliver you from this, and make you a king among kings, but you must not forget me," said the voice as if it were now hovering over Ryan's crouched body.

"I will never forget you. You are the savior. You are everything to me," Ryan said as tears flowed from his eyes.

"Rise now, and finish this journey, and all to come in God's name," the voice explained in a thunderous tone that made Ryan rise to his feet.

"I love you God," Ryan proclaimed as he stepped forward, noticing that morning had arrived.

Following a rhythm of step, step, kneel, rest, and then step again, Ryan moved steadily for the next hour. His strength was diminishing quickly, yet he still moved forward as fast as he could.

A bell tolled in the distance as Ryan began to fall to the ground; another bell rang out shortly after the first. Ryan started to crawl, inch by inch forward. A distant chorus of voices could be heard.

"In the morning, in the evening, throughout the day, and the night, God loves me, yes he does, God loves me, yes he does," sang the choir from the top of the mountain.

Ryan pushed himself up, and took seven more steps, finally reaching a point on the mountain where he could see the top. The glass church reflected the morning sunlight in millions of rays across the sky. Ryan pushed forward toward the choir ensemble only 50 feet in front of him.

"When I was down, when I was out, when I had nothing but doubt, he loved me, yes he loved me, yes he did," sang the choir as the members swayed back and forth in two lines facing each other in front of the church.

Channeling energy from an unknown source, Ryan walked toward the choir. His clothes soaked in mud, dry blood caked all over his arms, and Caroline's long hair and limp body across his shoulders, he walked forward.

"Oh my, someone get the pastor, get the pastor!" a choir member yelled out, breaking their song as she saw Ryan approaching.

Pastor Auggie Brown wasted no time in running toward Ryan after being alerted to the situation.

"Sir, are you OK? Are you alright? What happened?" Auggie yelled as he reached out his arms, catching Ryan's falling body, along with Caroline's and Becker's that fell with his.

The arriving congregation rushed to call an ambulance. The church videographer let his camera run as the pastor knelt over the three of them and prayed.

Chapter 54: ICU

A faint voice came from an intercom calling Nurse Evans to the intensive care unit. A waiting room filled with police and choir members flanked the intensive care unit. Anyone having to go to ICU had to first pass through the waiting area, forcing nurse Evans to wonder what she would find when she arrived at her destination.

"I've got two people badly dehydrated, one has a gunshot wound to the shoulder with severe blood loss, the other looks to be in coma. I'm going to need you to stay here with them while we get the operating room ready," Doctor Peter Hong explained as the nurse stood silently looking over them.

Nurse Evans began to prepare them as she did with any other unconscious patients by undressing them, cleaning off the debris from their bodies, and putting them into hospital robes. As she took the bag off Ryan's back, she noticed a white dog panting heavily inside the bag. She immediately unzipped it and called for help.

"Sue, get in here, can you get this dog to the emergency vet next door?" Nurse Evans asked as she continued to prep Caroline and Ryan for the doctor.

Caroline's eyes gently opened and closed twice, alerting the nurse that she was still alive.

"Doctor Hong, please come in here, you need to see this," Nurse Evans shouted as she tried to remain calm.

Chapter 55: Spoken Word

A small TV mounted to the corner of a wall in a room with two beds in the St. Bethany of Santa Barbara hospital hummed a jingle followed by drums that signaled to the residents of the hospital it was time for the news.

"Topping our newscast tonight is the incredible story of two hikers that nearly lost their life on Founder's Peak this past weekend. Reporting live from the glass church atop the mountain is senior reporter Jill Franklin—Jill," exclaimed the male anchor of the show in a calm, deep voice.

"Well, Bob, what happened on this mountain was nothing less than incredible. Two young people set forth on what they thought was a peaceful vacation, only to come face to face with a convicted serial killer," Jill Franklin of KLJ News 7 reported.

Caroline's eyes glanced at the television from her hospital bed as she felt a hand touch her shoulder.

"Its OK sweetheart, we are here now," Caroline's father said to her in a soft, comforting voice.

"We got here as soon as we could," Caroline's mother said, chiming into the conversation.

Caroline lay quietly on the hospital bed watching the television flash a picture of her face from high school, and a picture of Ryan's face from his job at the Columbus Tribune.

The daylight penetrated the curtains in a way that kept Caroline's eyes from closing for more than a few minutes at a time. Cards and flowers littered the shelves around Caroline's bed. A manila tray held several scoops of generic food on a plate that hadn't been touched since it arrived.

"Ryan, where is Ryan?" Caroline mumbled as her father darted toward the bed.

"Did you say something honey, baby, sweetheart, did you say something?" Caroline's father asked in an urgent tone as if it were the first words to ever leave her mouth.

Caroline shifted in her bed, moving her slender body up on the pillow. She swallowed twice, and took a deep breath.

"Where is Ryan?" Caroline whispered in a long and unnerving tone that seemed to seep out of her mouth like in a rattlesnake-like hiss.

"That boy, the one you went to the mountain with? Is that who you are talking about?" Caroline's father asked as he leapt up from the bed to find the answer.

"Go find out Jim, OK? Can you please go find out what happened to Ryan," Caroline's mother pleaded as she started to tear up from hearing her daughter's pain-ridden voice for the first time since the incident.

Jim Hempheart moved quickly from the hospital room down the hallway to a crescent desk manned by a security guard.

"Excuse me sir, can you tell me how to get in touch with Nurse Evans?" Jim Hempheart asked as calmly as he could.

"Sure, you are the guy from 306 right? I'll send her down to see you," the security guard said without budging.

Jim Hempheart returned to the room and explained the situation to Caroline's mother, Margret Hempheart.

Five minutes passed and with a quick knock, Nurse Evans entered the room.

"My daughter spoke, she just spoke, and she wants to know where Ryan is. Can you help us answer this question for her?" Jim said as he began to tear up himself.

Nurse Evans immediately pulled out a clipboard from the foot of Caroline's bed and noted the new developments in a scribbling motion that only nurses and doctors seem to perfect.

"Ryan is down the hall. He's in stable condition right now. We believe he is going to make it," Nurse Evans explained in a diplomatic tone that suggested everyone needed to calm down a bit.

A single tear fell from Caroline's face as she closed her eyes and let her head fall deep into the pillow underneath it.

Chapter 56: Home Again

Sandra gently folded Caroline's blanket over her bed as she declared victory in cleaning up the messy room. Every item of Caroline's had been organized, stowed, cleaned, and placed in an area that wasn't part of the floor. Even Caroline's pictures of Becker that had been pinned up to her bulletin board had been cleaned and framed in silver and black postcard-sized frames. Each picture was neatly hung on the wall, aligned perfectly with the next.

Sandra rushed down the stairs and pulled a fresh bag of kettle corn from the microwave, Caroline's favorite. She poured the bag into a sparkling white plastic bowl, and took a cheese grater to a series of caramel pieces, shaving them on top of the hot from the microwave popcorn.

The door opened, and Caroline walked in slowly, accompanied by her mother and father, the flashes from the media outside her house nearly blinding Sandra.

"Oh my goodness, I have missed you so much. Are you OK? Can I help you? Want some kettle corn? I made it for you," Sandra blurted out to Caroline and her parents as she made her way into the home.

"Hey Sandra, that's sweet of you, I'm OK for now, I think I

just want to go upstairs," Caroline said with a smile as she slowly worked her way up the stairs and into her room.

"Is she OK?" Sandra asked Caroline's parents, not knowing what their response would be.

"Yeah, she is going to be fine, she just needs some time to get a sense of normalcy back in her life, so please just try to be as normal around her as possible," Jim Hempheart said with a smile and a nod.

"We are going to go to the store to get a few things for her. Just keep an eye on her for us, OK?" Margaret Hempheart asked as she made her way toward the front door of the house.

"Yes ma'am, you got it," Sandra said as loud as she could without yelling.

Caroline's parents walked out the door, and pushed through the throngs of media reporters and cameramen to their car.

Sandra stood silent in the middle of the living room, feeling like someone that was in over her head. She moved toward the window, slid the blinds an inch and a half to the side and peered at the sea of unending members of the media outside. The only thing making them look as if there was some end in sight were the line of satellite trucks on the road behind them. Even though the door was shut, they still shouted questions, hoping to elicit some kind of response.

Sandra moved away from the window, and walked up the stairs. She thought about Caroline's parents asking her to keep an eye on Caroline for them. She figured it would be alright to check in on her roommate to see if she was doing OK.

Two quick rolls of the knuckles across Caroline's door is all it took for Caroline to give clearance.

"Come in," Caroline said softly.

"Hey, I just wanted to make sure you are doing alright," Sandra said before entering Caroline's room.

Sandra walked in softly, looking around the room that remained untouched since Caroline's arrival except for one duffle bag that sat unopened in the middle of Caroline's floor.

Caroline lay on top of the made bed fully clothed with her shoes on in silence.

"There are a lot of people out there. I guess they want to know how you are doing. Is there anything I can tell them? I mean is there anything you want me to tell them?" Sandra nervously asked Caroline as she gazed over her friend lying still on the bed.

Caroline sat quietly for a minute, motionless, and then opened her eyes softly and looked at Sandra.

"Thank God," Caroline said softly as she clutched a picture over her heart of Ryan and Becker smiling in a hospital bed that had the words "Get Well Soon" written on it in red marker.